Long-distance Love

"Mail call!" Louise said cheerfully as she came into the room.

"What is there?" Caitlin asked.

"Well, if you're wondering if there's a letter from Jed, there isn't. Sorry," Louise commiserated. "I would have given it to you right away. It's been a couple of weeks since you've gotten a letter, hasn't it?"

"Yes." Caitlin smiled weakly. "It's not that I'm worried. He's probably had a lot of studying to do," she said, making excuses for Jed.

"Uh-huh. Well, all I know is that you've been up to your eyeballs in activities and studies. But you still managed to find time to write to him. Maybe I shouldn't say this, Caitlin, but aren't you starting to get a little worried? I mean—you know, it's the guy who usually bails out of a long-distance relationship first. They're just weaker, that's all."

"Jed is not weak!" Caitlin objected.

"If you say so. It's just that I think you should be dating other guys. There are certainly tons of guys who want to ask you out. And they're *here*," Louise said with emphasis, "not two thousand miles away where you can't keep an eye on them."

PROMISES BROKEN

Caitlin

PROMISES
BROKEN

Created by
Francine Pascal

Written by
Diana Gregory

BANTAM BOOKS
TORONTO • NEW YORK • LONDON • SYDNEY • AUCKLAND

RL 6, IL age 12 and up

PROMISES BROKEN
A Bantam Book / December 1986

Conceived by Francine Pascal

Produced by Cloverdale Press Inc.

ISBN 0-553-26156-8

Published simultaneously in the United States and Canada

PRINTED IN THE UNITED STATES OF AMERICA

O   0 9 8 7 6 5 4 3 2 1

PROMISES
BROKEN

1

"Flight two-sixteen now arriving at gate number nine." The metallic voice came from somewhere overhead.

He's here, Caitlin thought. *Jed is actually here!* He had called her a few nights before to tell her he had a surprise for her. He had talked his father into letting him travel to Virginia to visit her before they both went off to college. Now, as Caitlin stood at the viewing window, she was so excited and happy that she couldn't stop herself from smiling. In minutes Jed would be walking through the gate at the far end of the main waiting area.

Caitlin turned from the viewing window and joined the growing crowd at the gate. A few passengers were just beginning to file through. She spotted Jed a few minutes later. Her heart pounded wildly at the familiar sight of his tall, trim body and ruggedly handsome face, deeply tanned from a summer of riding on the range. She called out to him.

"Jed!"

Hearing her, he turned, trying to pick her out in the crowd. Catching sight of her, he smiled and waved, as well as he could, since he was weighed down with his carry-on luggage. Changing course, he strode directly to her.

"Hi!" she greeted him softly.

"Hi!" He stood, looking down into her shining blue eyes for a long moment, grinning that engaging crooked smile that always made Caitlin's heart do a flip-flop. Then, dropping his suit bag and small canvas case to the floor, he swept her into his arms and buried his head in the thick, fragrant mass of her black hair as he hugged her to him. Gently tilting up her head so that their lips met, he kissed her.

As their lips parted, she looked up and saw the twinkle in his green eyes.

"There," he said. "I've been thinking of doing that ever since I left Denver."

"Oh?" she teased. "Not until then?"

"Well, okay"—he grinned—"maybe a few miles before Denver. Like back at the ranch this morning when I first woke up."

"That's much better." She laughed lightly.

After hugging her once more, he bent to retrieve his bags, and they began walking toward the down escalator.

Caitlin glanced at what he was carrying and asked, "Do you have any other luggage? Should we be heading for the claims area?"

"Huh-uh." He hefted the strap of the canvas bag onto his shoulder. "What you see is what I brought." He made a wry face. "And now that I see the way you're dressed, I'm not so sure about the stuff I packed. I forgot how hot it is here in Virginia."

"Oh," she said, "so that's why you're wearing a jacket."

"Yeah." He grinned. "We come from two different worlds."

"But they're only a few hours apart," she reminded him. As they walked, she leaned her head against the padded shoulder of his jacket for a second, inhaling the faint smell of sagebrush that still clung to the rough fabric. "I guess that means you didn't bring a bathing suit?" She raised her head to see him nod. "That's okay. Grandmother always has extra ones in the pool house. I'm sure we can find one that'll fit you." She gave him a stern look. "But you did bring your tennis gear, didn't you?"

"I sure did." He moved slightly away from her so they could start down the escalator. "Regulation whites." The corners of his mouth turned up in a slight smile. "Would I dare wear anything else around your grandmother? And I

3

brought a dinner jacket, too. I can't imagine a week at Ryan Acres without dressing for dinner at least once."

"Make that just about every night." She grimaced. "Grandmother's been doing a lot of entertaining lately. Colin is—" She stopped abruptly, shaking her head as if she didn't mean to say what she had started to. Jed raised a questioning eyebrow. "I'll tell you about him later," she responded. "Right now, I just want to concentrate on us."

They stepped off the escalator, and she tucked her hand into the crook of his arm. "Grandmother offered to have Rollins drive me in the Bentley, but I wanted to drive up myself. I didn't think you'd want to spend an hour in the back of a stuffy limo. So I've got the Z car. And I was lucky to find a parking space practically in front of the terminal." She squeezed his arm lightly, giving him a radiant smile at the same time. Then she said, "I thought this way we could take our time getting back to Ryan Acres."

To prove that she meant what she'd said— when she brought the bright red sports car to a stop at the end of the thirteen-mile-long access road leading away from Dulles Airport—she didn't take the Capital Beltway, which would have led them into the hunt country of Virginia and to her grandmother's estate and horse farm.

Instead, Caitlin chose to cross the Potomac River via the Theodore Roosevelt Bridge, heading into Washington, D.C. proper. Skirting the Lincoln Memorial and the Reflecting Pool, she drove on until she found a parking space near the Tidal Basin, only a little way from the Jefferson Memorial.

Getting out of the car, they walked to the entrance of the park. Jed had taken off his jacket and had slung it over his shoulder. They passed a hot dog vendor, and the smell of the roasting franks was too enticing to resist.

"Want one?" Jed asked. When Caitlin nodded, they turned back and stopped beneath the gaily striped umbrella. Jed ordered one for each of them.

"No onions, please," Caitlin told the man as he started to fork them on. When Jed told him to put them on his, she protested, "Don't you dare!"

The vendor smiled broadly and gave a knowing nod. "Ah, yes—lovers. Of course no onions for lovers."

Feeling happy, Caitlin returned the man's smile, then looked up at Jed. "See!"

"Okay, okay!" Jed laughed. "No onions, then."

They munched on the hot dogs as they walked along the edge of the Tidal Basin, in the shade of the famed cherry trees.

They had finished eating by the time they reached the bottom of the steps that led up to the Jefferson Memorial.

"If you climb to the top, there's a place where you can sit and look straight across at the Washington Monument and the White House," Caitlin said.

"Then let's do it," Jed replied, smiling. "Who could pass up a view like that?" Jed took her hand, and the two began the climb up the wide, shallow steps.

Reaching the top, they found several tourists walking along the inside aisle, between the closed rotunda and the row of massive, supporting columns that made up the facade of the graceful marble building. "What about here?" Jed suggested, gesturing toward one of the columns. Caitlin nodded, and they leaned against it. It was so large that they had a perfect feeling of privacy as they looked out over the beautiful body of water toward the White House in the distance.

"I really do love it up here." Caitlin spoke with a feeling of reverence. "I think Washington is my favorite city in the entire world."

"You like it even better than Paris, or Rome?"

"Much better! And when the cherry trees are in blossom—Oh, Jed, we've just got to come up next spring when they're—" Suddenly she stopped, a stricken look on her face. "I don't believe it. For a second, I forgot that you wouldn't be here in the spring. Oh, Jed, I can't make myself believe that you're going to spend a year at a college in Montana instead of here, where you'd planned to be."

"I know." Jed's voice was low and sounded unhappy as he spoke. "When I was out riding last week, I'd look around and realize suddenly that I wouldn't be seeing you for a year." He touched her hand. "Except, of course, for a couple of weeks at Christmas. And I think my dad only agreed to let me fly east then because he knew I wouldn't agree to go to Montana Agricultural at all. That, and he must have seen how miserable I was after you'd flown back home."

Jed's mouth tightened. "And I suppose he knew I might just take off without his permission—just so I could see you." Jed reached over and gently smoothed back one of the dark tendrils of Caitlin's hair that was blowing softly against her cheek.

"Oh, Jed." Caitlin moved her head so that she could look into his eyes. "Why don't you go ahead and defy him? Why don't you just stay here? You could transfer. It would be so easy. I mean, you were all enrolled at Carleton Hill until a couple of weeks ago. I'm sure they'd take

7

you back. After all, what good is one year at an agricultural college when you really want to study law?"

"You know I can't stay here, Caitlin. I've already promised my father that I'd try Montana Agricultural College for a year. And it *is* only for one year. If I still feel the same way about pursuing a law career after my freshman year, he's given his word that he'll never mention a ranching career to me again. Look, he just wants me to give myself the chance to get the experience I need to make an intelligent decision about what I'm going to do with my life."

"No, Jed. He just wants to keep you out there long enough to make you break down and stay there—to make you become the rancher he wants you to be."

"Maybe, Caitlin," Jed admitted. "Maybe that is it. But if it is, I can't really blame him. Of course he'd like to have the ranch stay in the family. He wants a partner—he needs one. He's getting old, you know."

"Okay, great." Caitlin's mouth twisted downward. "What about your sister? Or is your father so much of a chauvinist that he wouldn't want Melanie for a partner?"

"I'm afraid he is. He couldn't turn over control to a woman. Also, I don't know if Melanie would enjoy running a ranch."

"And you would! Is that what you're telling me?" Caitlin's eyes were narrowing slightly.

"I could if I didn't have something I wanted to do more," Jed said in an even tone.

"Are you really sure it's not what you want?" Something had happened to him over the summer, she thought as she regarded him. In some ways, he wasn't the boy she had fallen in love with when they were both students at Highgate Academy. Now he was a man. He had always been more mature and different from the eastern boys at school, but now she was startled by just how grown-up he was. She had spent the summer with him; the only time they had been separated were these past couple of weeks, after she had returned from her visit to his ranch. But he looked even more like a cowboy back in the East. "Jed, are you really sure?"

"Yes, Caitlin. Yes, I am!" Turning to her, he gently cupped her shoulders with his hands. "Of course I am," he reassured her. "I love you. What I want more than anything is to spend my life here—with you." Sighing slightly, he shook his head. "But, Caitlin, I can't deny that I love my father, too. And all he's asking is one year of my life. Only one year. That's all. And, if you love me as much as I hope you do, you won't make it any harder on me than necessary," he pleaded.

When she gazed into his eyes, she found herself getting so hopelessly lost in their emerald green depths, that all she could manage to murmur was, "Jed—Jed, I love you. I love you very much. I'll do whatever I can to help. And I'll try to be more patient and understanding."

"And I'll do anything for you," Jed replied as he pulled her into his arms. "And I will love you always. *Forever.*"

2

Jed stood up, walked to the edge of the pool, and dove in. A moment later he surfaced, then swam to the other end. Making a perfect racing turn, he headed back toward where Caitlin sat curled up on the plump flowered cushions of a chaise longue. She watched him, admiring the effortless way his strong, muscled arms sliced through the water. After several laps he reached the end nearest to her, rested for a moment, then hoisted himself out.

It had been three days since Caitlin met Jed at Dulles Airport. That meant there were only four days left before he would have to leave again. She drew her knees up and wrapped her arms around them, hugging her legs to her body. Only four more days!

Jed walked toward her, his feet making wet footprints on the flagstones. Picking up his towel, which lay at the foot of the chaise next to

Caitlin's, he blotted the water from his tanned shoulders and thighs.

He tossed the towel down, then flopped back on his chaise. "That felt great. You ought to go in."

"No, thanks," Caitlin answered lazily. "I think I'll just stay right here and work on my tan. Would you mind putting some lotion on my back? I think it's time to turn over." Sitting up, she handed him the bottle of suntan lotion and turned her back to him.

"Gladly." Uncapping the bottle, Jed poured a small amount of lotion into the palm of his hand. Then he began massaging it onto her back. As he did so, he compared the dark brown of his fingers to the golden apricot color of her smooth skin. She was so beautiful. He loved the way the dark, glossy mass of her hair lay against her shoulders, and how clean it smelled. And her waist, where his hand lingered, was so narrow that he could almost span it with both hands. He wanted to reach his hands around it and pull her back against his chest so he could kiss the slim column of her neck. Then he would plant a row of feather-light kisses along the delicate curve of her slender jaw—

A peal of laughter from the nearby tennis court interrupted his thoughts. He had nearly forgotten that Regina Ryan, Caitlin's grandmother, and her guest for the day, Colin Wollman, were playing there. The *thwock* of tennis balls being hit back and forth had been so constant that it had become only so much background noise.

Regina Ryan. Jed thought for a moment about Caitlin's grandmother. In spite of her silver hair, she still looked quite young. It would have been easy for someone to mistake her for Caitlin's mother. She had raised Caitlin after her daughter, Laura, had died during childbirth. She had schemed then that Caitlin would never know her father, telling her that he'd run off.

Jed could never really decide if it had been fate or coincidence that had brought Caitlin and her father together. Caitlin had been visiting a sick friend at the small hospital where her father was the director. When she'd met him, Dr. Gordon Westlake had noticed Caitlin's resemblance to his beloved Laura right away. But he had reasoned that it was impossible that there was any connection. Later, when he had discovered that Caitlin was a Ryan, he'd realized that his suspicions had been correct. Laura had been a Ryan, too.

Gordon Westlake confronted Regina Ryan with what he had found out, and finally she had admitted the truth. She had taken Laura to Europe to get her away from Gordon Westlake. There, Laura had discovered she was pregnant. When Laura died, Regina Ryan blamed Gordon

Westlake for her loss and kept Caitlin from him. But now father and daughter were making up for lost time, becoming closer every day.

Jed shook his head, taking his hand away from Caitlin's back and recapping the lotion bottle. He still didn't understand how Caitlin could have forgiven her grandmother, and he wasn't at all sure he'd have been able to if it had been him.

Jed tossed the bottle on the foot of the chaise and settled back. "I'm beginning to see what you mean about Colin being here constantly. For a guy who's supposed to be attending to Ryan Mining's legal problems, he has an awful lot of time to do other things."

"I told you." Caitlin made an unpleasant face before lying down on her stomach and resting her head on her hands. "He may as well have moved in here. He's been here for dinner at least four times this week. Some days he even uses the library for an office. And he and grandmother go out almost constantly—if not to the theater, then to parties or something. Grandmother says he's only doing his job, but I don't remember her old attorney coming to the house except to drop off papers or to attend business dinners."

"Do you suppose he's got more on his mind than business? I mean, maybe there's a little love interest there, too," Jed suggested.

"Yes." Caitlin raised her head to look at him. "That's exactly what I've been thinking. But I've also been trying to convince myself that I'm wrong. After all, Colin's in his forties, and my grandmother is—"

"Still very attractive," Jed finished for her. "Maybe she is older than he is. That doesn't seem to matter nowadays. And she's so active."

"You're right about that." Caitlin nodded. "I don't mind her being interested in a man. It's who the man is. I don't like Colin one bit; and you know I've *never* liked him. And then when he put us down when we tried to convince my grandmother to do something to improve the mining conditions at Rock Ridge, I truly disliked him."

"Well, you're not going to get an argument from me about Colin Wollman being a class-A creep." Jed's eyes narrowed as he remembered back to earlier that summer. He and Caitlin had been part of a service project in which they and a couple of other students from Highgate Academy—the boarding school they'd both graduated from—had spent four weeks organizing and running a play school in a mining town called Rock Ridge. The mines in that town belonged to Mrs. Ryan. During their month there, a couple of the miners' wives had told them about some safety problems. Jed had then done a huge amount of research into the government regulations, which were barely adequate, and put together a complete report. He and Caitlin had shown the report to Mrs. Ryan and just about convinced her to look into the violations they had found when Colin showed up. He had pointed out that Jed and Caitlin were too young and inexperienced to really know what they were talking about. He had done such a good job of putting them in their place that Mrs. Ryan had gone over to his side almost immediately.

"Speaking of Rock Ridge," Caitlin said, sitting up and swinging her legs around so that she was facing him, "I almost forgot to tell you about the letter that was waiting for me when I got home from Montana. It was from Lola Butler. You remember her, don't you?"

"How could I forget? She was one of the miners' wives who helped us set up the project." Jed nodded. "So, what was the letter about?"

"Mainly to thank us for all the work we did, and to say that Emily was doing a wonderful job continuing the school." Emily Michaels was Jed's cousin. She and a couple of other Highgate students had kept the play running for the rest of the summer. "A lot of the mothers got involved, too. So I guess we really did do some good out there."

"That is great news."

"But she also wrote something else. Something I didn't understand. She apologized for the run-in you had with Kathy Stokes's brother. She hoped you wouldn't think badly of the rest of the people in Rock Ridge because of that." Caitlin frowned slightly. "Do you have any idea what she meant? I didn't even know you'd met Kathy's brother."

"Um-hmm." Without really answering, Jed shrugged, closed his eyes against the sun, and leaned back against the headrest.

He remembered all right. How could he ever forget that day he and Jake had clashed? His sister Kathy had been a favorite of Caitlin's—bright and cheerful with a round face and huge gray eyes. On her last day at Rock Ridge, Caitlin had brought one of her favorite old dolls and had asked Jed to take it to Kathy's house to give it to her. But when he had arrived at the isolated cabin, he was met at the door by Kathy's older brother, a boy about three or four years older than he was. Jed would also never forget the look of absolute hatred that flashed in the boy's slate-colored eyes. When Jed had tried to hand the doll through the door to Kathy, her brother had snatched it from him. Then he had viciously smashed the doll against the porch post, shattering the delicate porcelain head into tiny pieces.

Jake had then flung himself furiously at Jed, his fists flailing. The fight had not lasted long. Though taken by surprise, Jed had the advantage of a cooler head and had walked away a few minutes later with only a bruised jaw. Kathy's brother, on the other hand, had been left sitting dazedly on the ground, holding his head.

"Jed"—Caitlin shook his arm—"you're not telling the truth, I can tell. Something bad did happen, didn't it?"

Jed opened his eyes but didn't look at her. "It wasn't any big deal."

But Caitlin wouldn't give up. "What are you hiding?" she insisted. She tightened her hold on his arm. "Jed, you know that not telling the whole truth is just as bad as lying, don't you? Besides, I have a right to know if something really terrible happened in Rock Ridge. I was the one in charge of the project."

"Oh, all right!" Jed sat up. "Listen, I meant it when I said that it was no big deal. And I sure don't know how Lola Butler found out." He shook his head. "Do you remember that last day, when you asked me to take that doll out to the Stokes's cabin to give to Kathy?" Caitlin nodded. "Well, her brother was there. And I guess he thought giving Kathy the doll was some sort of act of charity. He didn't like the idea very much, so he took a swing at me."

"You mean there was a fight?" Caitlin's eyes widened.

"More like a small scuffle."

"No. You mean a fight."

"Look, Caitlin, were you there?"

"No." She shook her head. Then she remembered the slight bruise Jed had had on his face after they left Rock Ridge. He had been in a real fight. But, Caitlin realized, there was no point in trying to make him admit it if he hadn't by then.

"Take my word for it, Caitlin. It was just a scuffle." Jed lay back against the cushions again and closed his eyes. "Now you know the truth, so let's just forget about it, okay? I'm not exactly proud of what happened."

"But, Jed, you were only defending yourself."

"I don't care. I hate violence. I don't think anything's ever been settled by one person beating up another person."

"But—"

"End of discussion!" Jed said flatly. "Now, let's either talk about something else or go do something. As far as I'm concerned, Kathy's big brother is very old news. He's out of our lives, and I think we should forget him."

Caitlin started to open her mouth in further protest, but she decided it would be better if she waited until later to pursue the subject further. Surely, sometime in the next few days, she would find the perfect time for it.

The last four days slipped by, however, filled with tennis, swimming, a visit to Jed's cousin Emily, and long horseback rides through the rolling countryside of Ryan Acres and the woods beyond.

One afternoon they took a long drive, exploring narrow, rarely used roads and finding places neither of them had seen before. They had taken a picnic lunch and stopped to eat it by a small stream, spreading out a blanket in the shade of a stately old oak tree. After lunch Caitlin leaned back against the tree, cradling Jed's head in her lap. He told her about his dreams for their future while Caitlin wove a wreath of multicolored late-summer flowers. It had been a time of love, not at all right to bring up anything unpleasant, such as Jed's fight with Kathy's brother.

On Jed's last day at Ryan Acres, they drove over to Charlottesville so that Jed could see Monticello, the home of Thomas Jefferson.

"You kissed me on the steps of the Jefferson Memorial," Caitlin said teasingly. "It's only fitting that we visit his home so you can kiss me there, too."

And Jed did, in the doorway of the tiny building Jefferson had had built behind the main house. The cozy structure had served as the honeymoon cottage for him and his wife. "Maybe we should make this a tradition," Jed suggested, lightly running his finger down her nose, then leaning forward to kiss the tip of it.

"Hmmm." Caitlin smiled. "I think I like that idea."

"What about every Fourth of July?" Jed suggested. "Very appropriate, don't you think?"

"Very." Caitlin giggled softly, then kissed him back lightly.

They had lunch at an old Colonial inn nearby. As they sat across from each other at a scarred wooden table, their waiter, wearing period knee breeches and a puffy-sleeved white muslin shirt, told them that the tables and high-backed warming benches by the fireplace dated to the time of the Revolution—and that Thomas Jefferson himself had eaten many a meal at the inn.

The beef stew and biscuits they were served were delicious if a bit heavy for a warm late-summer day. A note on the menu explained that both had been prepared from recipes that dated back to the Revolution. But Caitlin could hardly eat more than a few bites. She kept stealing glances at Jed, sadly counting the hours and minutes until she drove him to Dulles so that he could catch his plane. Even though she understood his reasons, she hated Jed's father for taking him from her.

"A quarter for your thoughts," Jed said.

"Hmmm—what?" She gave a small start.

"Well, a penny doesn't seem like quite enough." He smiled warmly. "You had this faraway look in your eyes. I couldn't help wondering what you were thinking about."

She gave a slight shake of her head, feeling embarrassed at having been caught thinking such thoughts. The last thing she wanted to admit to Jed was how she felt about his stern and rigid father. "Oh, nothing really," she said vaguely. Picking up her fork, she pushed at a piece of carrot on her plate. "Mostly I was thinking about college. You know, what to bring with me. The dorm rooms at Carleton Hill aren't very big. My roommate is a sophomore, so she probably has a lot of stuff from last year."

"Well, at least she can show you the ropes."

"That's what I thought, too," Caitlin agreed. "But, on the other hand, it might be nice to have a freshman to room with—someone to commiserate with."

"That's true." Jed broke off a piece of biscuit and buttered it. "I have no idea who my roommate is. I think we get assigned rooms after we get there. It's a really informal school, and not very large. As for packing, all I have to do is stuff my jeans and boots into my bag and I'm off. Any parties they have are strictly casual. And there are no fraternities, no football team. Just an occasional rodeo."

"Boy, that sure is different from Carleton Hill. I think one of the reasons my grandmother approved of my going there is because of Carleton's social life. She thinks I'll meet all the 'right people.'" Caitlin gave Jed a knowing look. "But I still haven't made up my mind whether or not I want to join a sorority."

"Oh, boy!" Jed grinned. "I can imagine what your grandmother would say if she could hear you say that. I'll bet she'd consider that pretty close to blasphemy."

"You're probably right." Caitlin grinned back. "She's already reminding me to register for rush week. If I do decide not to join a sorority, I'm not quite sure how I'm going to explain it to her."

"Maybe it would be simpler to join."

"Maybe it would." Caitlin laughed. Suddenly the laughter died away. "Oh, Jed." She sighed. "It's such a long time until Christmas. How can I exist that long without you?"

"You will," Jed said sternly. "You'll do just fine. Just keep thinking, as I'm going to, that Christmas vacation is less than four months away."

Less than four months—less than four months. Caitlin kept repeating those words over and over to herself the next morning as she stood at the airport, watching while Jed's plane took off and disappeared into the Washington haze.

Finally, when she could no longer see it, she turned and made her way out of the terminal. Tears stung her eyes. But she would wait as patiently as she could, she promised herself. She would write to Jed every day, and there would be phone calls. She would throw herself into her studies to keep her mind occupied. But she knew it would be difficult. She missed him already.

3

"You are joking, aren't you, Caitlin?" Louise
Bates, Caitlin's new roommate, had a look of
disbelief on her face. She had just finished
hanging her favorite print on the wall, and now
she plopped down on her unmade bed. "You
don't seriously mean you're planning to go
through your entire freshman year without a
single date, do you?" She shook her head.
"Caitlin, that's social suicide."

Caitlin was sitting cross-legged on the floor in
front of a low bookcase, rearranging her books.

Caitlin's side of the room already reflected her
personality. Caitlin had spent the past week at
school for freshman orientation week and was
pretty much settled in. Unlike her room at
Highgate, which had been furnished by a pro-
fessional decorator her grandmother had hired,
Caitlin had picked out everything for her college
dorm room by herself. Mrs. Ryan just hadn't had
the time to argue. *I guess this is one time I should be*

thankful that Grandmother's seeing so much of Colin Wollman, Caitlin thought wryly. *He does keep her awfully busy.*

Caitlin's room at Carleton was old and charming. It had odd angles, lots of wood paneling, and even a window seat on Caitlin's side of the room. She had filled the window seat with ruffled, pastel pillows, and sheer, white curtains hung above. Her bedspread was also white, with a pattern of tiny bunches of forget-me-nots on it. And over the end of the neatly made bed lay a folded quilt in shades of lavender and moss green.

At Louise's outburst, Caitlin had put down the book she was holding. She looked at her roommate and smiled easily. "I think I'll live without dating. Besides, I love my boyfriend very much, and I can't imagine going out with anyone else while we're apart."

"Not even to football games and rallies and fraternity parties? What are you going to do on Friday and Saturday nights?"

"Write letters, I guess," Caitlin responded. "And study"

"You'll end up being an outcast, you know. Listen, Caitlin, I know what I'm talking about. Freshman year is supposed to be fun. I had an absolute ball last year. I'll bet I had more dates than any other freshman. And the parties never stopped. You don't want to miss that, do you?

Don't you know that this school is known for its hunks?" She leaned forward, resting her elbows on her knees. "The fraternities even got together last year and did a calendar of the best-looking guys on campus to raise money for some charity. It sold out on the first day! *That's* how gorgeous they are."

"Sounds tempting." Caitlin smiled. "But I'm not going to change my mind."

"Even for the mixer next weekend? No one goes in couples, and it's not a date thing at all. Really. It's just so everyone can get to know everyone else."

"Sorry."

"I know, I know. You'll be busy writing that letter." Louise made a face. Pushing herself off the bed, she went over to Caitlin's dresser. A framed photograph of Jed was sitting on top of it. It was a casual shot, taken during the summer at the ranch. Jed's hat was pushed to the back of his head, and he was leaning against a fence post, his arms folded across his chest. With his tanned face and crooked, boyish smile, he looked vulnerable yet somehow confident as well. "This is Jed, isn't it?" Louise asked as she picked up the silver frame.

"Um-hmm." Caitlin drew her knees up to her chest and leaned her chin on them. "Wouldn't you say he's worth waiting for?"

"He's definitely adorable," Louise admitted.

"But I'll also bet you that he's not going to waste *his* freshman year sitting around his dorm room out there in Wyoming waiting for letters from you. Not if I know guys the way I think I do."

"Well, you don't know Jed," Caitlin said. "And it's Montana, not Wyoming."

"Whatever." Louise shrugged. "All those square-shaped states out there look alike to me." She put Jed's picture back on Caitlin's dresser. "I think I'll run down and check the mail. When I get back, want to head over to the student union for a soda? We'll be spending enough time in this room after classes start—at least I know *you* will!" she said pointedly.

"Sounds good," Caitlin replied easily, unperturbed by Louise's remark.

"Great. See you in a few minutes."

After Louise had gone, Caitlin sat and looked at her books. She realized that one of them wasn't hers. It belonged to Ginny Brookes, her best friend and roommate from Highgate. Although Louise seemed nice enough, Caitlin knew she was going to miss Ginny. Idly, she ran one finger along the spine of the book. In the four years they had roomed together at boarding school, they had become very close—close enough to share their innermost secrets. She sighed. Now she would have to start with someone new.

Louise was the complete opposite of Ginny.

Ginny was athletic and completely at ease in any sport but shy around boys. Louise had already admitted that sports were not her thing—but boys were. Apparently her philosophy was, the more the better. And Caitlin could easily imagine that Louise didn't have any problem attracting them—not with her figure and long, honey-colored silken hair that fell straight to the middle of her back.

Caitlin smiled. Louise reminded her of how she used to be before she met Jed: boy crazy. Perhaps she and Louise would hit it off after all.

Caitlin thought about that morning when she had first met Louise. The sophomores, juniors, and seniors had arrived back on campus that day. Dressed in worn jeans and a white, button-down shirt that was several sizes too big for her, Louise had looked every inch the college student. Her light hair was pulled up in a ponytail.

"Hi, you must be Caitlin," she had said. Her tone was friendly, but somehow Caitlin detected a false note in it—as if she were only trying to be polite.

"Yes, I am. And you're Louise?" Caitlin had ventured.

Louise's father had followed, carrying several suitcases. She, her father, and a couple of male friends of Louise's had brought in box after box of Louise's belongings.

After everyone had left, Louise regarded the

suitcases and boxes. "Listen, Caitlin, I can't stand to unpack now. I think I'll go and find out if some of my friends are back. I'll unpack later."

She ran her hand down her ponytail. "Do you need anything?" she had asked.

"No," Caitlin had replied, a little surprised that Louise was going to leave so quickly.

"Great." Louise grabbed her purse and turned to leave. "I'll see you later," she called out airily.

"Okay. 'Bye," Caitlin had said.

Now, as she waited for Louise to come back from checking the mail, Caitlin found herself really hoping they'd become friends. It would be terrible to have to go through a year of college living with someone she didn't like.

Caitlin thought about Ginny and how much she would love to see her. They hadn't had a chance to get together since graduation.

She was glad Ginny had decided not to go to Brown and had decided instead on the University of Virginia, which wasn't that far away. Maybe she would call her and invite her to come up. Not the coming weekend because Ginny would probably still be settling in, but the next one. Yes, Caitlin decided, she would definitely call Ginny in the next couple of days.

When Louise returned, Caitlin quickly changed into khaki walking shorts and a blue oxford-cloth shirt. She ran a brush through her hair so that it lay in dark, shining waves on her shoulders. Taking some money from her wallet, she shoved it into the back pocket of her shorts. Then she was ready.

"Good enough for the student union?" she asked.

"More than good enough," Louise replied. "Maybe I should change, too." Louise was wearing jeans and a Carleton Hill University T-shirt, but her wholesome beauty made up for her casual clothing. She was the kind of girl who could make even the most ordinary clothes look elegant.

"Don't be silly. You look great," Caitlin assured her truthfully. "I was feeling grungy from the heat, or I wouldn't have changed myself."

"Well—if you're sure?"

"Sure I'm sure." Smiling, Caitlin headed toward the door. "Now come on. I'm dying of thirst."

The girls' dorm was located on the eastern edge of the campus, about a block from fraternity row. To get to the student union—the huge building that housed the book store, TV and game lounges, dining rooms, and a small coffee shop, along with other shops that sold everything from sweatshirts to posters—Louise and Caitlin cut straight across the campus toward the center, past the library and and the main administration building.

The architecture of the university was mainly

Georgian; the buildings were stately and elegant, made of darkened red brick, with white wooden trim and shutters; the walks that wound throughout the well-maintained grounds were brick as well. The weather was still very warm. All along the paths the flowers continued to bloom in perfectly maintained beds. The grass was manicured, and the air was heavy with the scent of many flowers.

They had just passed the corner of the administration building when they heard footsteps behind them.

"Louise! Louise Bates!" a strong, masculine voice called. "Is that you?"

Halting, Louise spun around. A pleased expression crossed her face. "Darrell Hart. Why, hello there! I didn't expect to see you back here. How are you?"

"Great, now that I've seen you." The husky, blond-haired boy came up and slung a muscular arm around Louise's shoulder. By his build, Caitlin was sure he was a football player.

"What happened to Yale?" Louise asked in a confiding tone.

"I decided I couldn't possibly transfer to Yale if you weren't going to be there to cheer for me." His gray eyes looked at her devilishly. "So here I am."

"And am I ever glad. How could Carleton possibly continue to exist without you?" She smiled up at him. Then, remembering Caitlin, she turned to introduce her. "Caitlin, I'd like you to meet one of those hunks I told you about. This is Darrell Hart."

"Hi!" Caitlin said warmly. "It's nice to meet you."

"Whoa!" Darrell's eyes widened as he looked at Caitlin for the first time. "Am I ever glad to meet *you*." He flashed her the kind of smile Caitlin was sure had a lot to do with him being regarded as a hunk. "Where have you been all my life?" Dropping his arm from Louise's shoulders, he took a few steps closer to Caitlin. "You have the most gorgeous blue eyes. Has anyone ever told you that?"

Is this guy for real? Caitlin wondered. She didn't know whether to laugh or say thank you. She was deciding what to say, when Louise did it for her.

"Honestly, Darrell! How full of corn can you get? Where did you spend your summer, in Iowa?"

But it was as if Darrell hadn't heard her. Still looking straight into Caitlin's eyes, he asked, "Where are you two headed?"

"To the union," Caitlin replied. "We're going for a Coke."

"Great," Darrell said. "I've just developed a huge thirst. Mind if I join you?"

"Ummm—" Caitlin hesitated, wanting to say

no. He was coming on too strong, but she had just met him, and he was Louise's friend. It would sound impolite if she said she did mind.

"Yes, we do mind," Louise said almost curtly. Moving so that she was between Darrell and Caitlin, she linked her arm through Caitlin's and added more cheerfully, "It's just going to be girl talk. No guys allowed." But she was fuming as she thought, *at least no guys who aren't one hundred percent loyal to me.* Outwardly, she smiled at Caitlin. "Right?"

"Right," Caitlin agreed, feeling relieved. More and more she was starting to think that she and Louise were going to get along just fine. Louise had obviously picked up on the fact that she hadn't been too thrilled at the thought of having Darrell join them. "You'd really be bored, Darrell. Louise promised to fill me in on school stuff." She made a bored face. "See, it's nothing that would interest you." Then, giving him a warm smile. "But it was nice meeting you. And I'm sure I'll see you around."

"A lot, I hope." Darrell flashed his perfect smile at Caitlin again before he began backing away. "And trust me, I'll definitely keep my eyes open for you." Just before he turned to jog away, he added, almost as an afterthought, "Oh, yeah, nice seeing you again, Louise."

"Good-looking," Caitlin ventured after he'd gone. "Did you go out with him last year?"

"For a while," Louise replied evenly. "But I think he's changed over the summer. I don't think I'm going to be seeing much of him this year."

"He did come on a bit strong."

Louise's eyes narrowed. "He sure did."

Twenty minutes later, as they sat across from each other in a large booth in the student union coffee shop, it became clear to Caitlin that Louise must have been one of the most popular girls on campus the previous year. At least ten guys had already stopped by their table to say hello. And now four of them were coming back, drinks in hand, to join them.

It wasn't long before Caitlin was feeling perfectly at ease with them. One, a redheaded boy named Josh Weston, had a terrific sense of humor. She found herself laughing as he described the freshman courses to watch out for. He was cute, as were the others. But not one of them came even close to Jed, she thought. Still, it felt good to be part of a lively crowd again. She was having fun.

Louise, however, was not. In fact, as the minutes passed and everyone's attention shifted away from her more and more, she began to feel out of it. She couldn't believe what was happening to her. The previous spring, two of those guys had almost had a fistfight over who would buy her a hamburger. *Now look at them*, she thought resentfully. They had their backs turned to her and were almost drooling over Caitlin.

She leaned back against the high wooden seat, and glared at Caitlin. She didn't think her new roommate was all that pretty. But these guys seemed to think so. Well, forget them. Who needed them, anyway? She sure didn't. There were plenty more where they came from. But then she suddenly remembered how Darrell Hart had gotten all dewy-eyed over Caitlin, and Darrell was hardly what you'd call a jerk. Well *damn* Caitlin—

All at once, Louise realized that someone was watching her—someone across the room. Without turning her head, she looked over to see who it was. Her gaze was met by one of the most gorgeous guys she had ever seen. He had very dark hair, incredible gray eyes, and a chiseled face. But it was the sensitivity in his face that drew her attention most of all. He looked kind and understanding, yet absolutely sure of himself. She could have looked at him forever. But Louise knew she had to do something. She couldn't simply sit there staring back at him.

She smiled.

But he didn't react, and she began to feel stupid. Perhaps he hadn't been looking at her after all. Then she noticed the corners of his mouth turn up, slowly at first, then into a smile that made her heart leap to her throat. She felt ridiculously pleased that she had been the one to bring that smile to his lips. Finally he turned away.

As Louise watched him become involved in a conversation with the other people at his table, she remembered then who he was. She had heard about him. His name was Julian Stokes and he was a senior, a premed major. He was also at Carleton Hill on some kind of a scholarship. She'd heard that he was brilliant.

"Hey, Louise! Louise, where are you?" Someone was touching her arm, trying to get her attention. She blinked.

"Hmmm?" Frowning, she turned to see Josh grinning at her. "What?"

"You looked as though you were a million miles away. Just thought you'd like to rejoin the group. Besides, we need your help with Caitlin."

"What do you mean? What kind of help?" She glanced at Caitlin, who shrugged and smiled back at her amiably.

Stan, the boy sitting next to Caitlin, said, "We're trying to convince her to go to the mixer on Friday night."

"Yeah," the boy on the other side of Caitlin spoke up. "So she'll have a chance to meet the right kind of guys."

Louise, seeing all the boys hovering over her roommate, felt like grinding her teeth. Instead, she laughed, hoping she sounded light and carefree. "Well, gee, guys, it doesn't look as though Caitlin really needs to go to the dance to meet the right kind of guys." She smiled at Caitlin. "It looks as though she's doing just fine right here."

4

"So what do you think, Julian?" the thin, dark-haired sophomore asked. He leaned forward, his eyes questioning. "Do you think I should switch majors?" Julian, he was sure, would come up with the right answer for him. He trusted Julian's insight and sensitivity about people. Yes, Julian would be able to put the whole thing in the right perspective.

"All right, Carl, tell me—" Julian paused, his gaze moving away momentarily. He looked again at the pretty blond across the room and at the girl sitting across from her. Then, he forced himself to concentrate on Carl's problem again. "What do *you* really want to do for a living when you get out of college? Never mind about what your uncle thinks you should do. He's not the one who has to live your life. You do. Try to see yourself ten years from now. Would you be better off as a stockbroker or a doctor?"

The sophomore scowled. "That's what I was hoping you could help me figure out."

"Well, maybe I could. But I don't think it's my place to do that." Julian's voice was soft. "It's a major decision, Carl—one you have to make for yourself. But you might start by asking yourself if you're ready to put in the time it takes to become a doctor. And it *does* take a long time, you know."

"Well, *you're* willing to spend those years. And—uh—doctors make a lot of money."

"Is that what's most important to you? Money?" Julian asked. "If it is, maybe you should think about becoming a stockbroker."

"You know, I think you're right, Julian—thanks!" The look in the boy's eyes was almost worshipful; Julian had helped him to see what he really wanted. Then, sounding a little embarrassed that his decision had come down to how he could make the most money, he said, "That's—that's what my uncle said, too. I guess he was right."

"I'm glad I could help, Carl." Julian leaned back in his chair, suggesting that he was dismissing Carl and taking himself out of the conversation that flowed around the table. Without their noticing, he looked around at the others. The ones who had become his—what? Followers? Yes, they were followers. It amused Julian that he could manipulate them so easily. If he had wanted to, he could have advised Carl to change his major from business to premed. And Carl probably would have done it, sticking it out until he became a doctor—a very bad one, no doubt.

Money! Carl had mentioned money, yet, he had also been embarrassed to admit it. Julian had seen the faint flush stain Carl's cheeks. Well, Carl was right. He just didn't know how right. How could he? Carl was from a rich family, while he— Julian shook his head. It was a good thing no one knew where he came from. If they did, they would never have accepted him as they had. Wealth—it counted for a lot!

Julian turned his head to look across the room again, this time at the girl sitting across from the pretty blond. *He looked at Caitlin Ryan.*

He had known for some time that she would be arriving at Carleton Hill as a freshman that fall. A girl of Caitlin Ryan's social prominence made the news even when she did something as commonplace as enrolling in college. It had been in the local papers. When he had read the articles about her, he had realized what a stroke of luck it was that she would be on the same campus with him. Caitlin Ryan—the person he had sworn revenge against—right there, at his mercy. And, best of all, she didn't know it. She didn't have the slightest idea who he was.

She might have recognized the name *Jake* Stokes if his sister Kathy had even mentioned his name to her during the summer when she had been enrolled in the play school program. Everyone in Rock Ridge called him by his nickname. But everyone at the university knew him by his real name, Julian. It would make it all so easy, he thought. His eyes narrowed as he watched her. She was so beautiful, but God, how he hated her.

Julian's mind went back, rolling away the years to the Christmas when he was ten and the high and mighty Mrs. Regina Ryan, owner of Ryan Mining, had come to Rock Ridge to give her token presents to the miners' children. Caitlin had come with her. It was the first time he had seen her. She was so perfect, in her little fur-collared coat and patent leather shoes, climbing daintily out of the rear of the limousine. She had stood there, looking like a princess. He, on the other hand, had felt every inch the poor, ragged miner's son, in his dirty jeans and torn sweater. His clothes were so threadbare that the biting wind blew right through them. The chauffeur had taken a stack of presents from the trunk and given them to Caitlin to hand out. But Julian hadn't wanted any dumb gift from the Ryans. It probably would have been useless anyway—a game, or something equally frivolous. Yet he had been drawn toward Caitlin. He had just wanted to touch the coat she was wearing; to see if the material was as soft as it looked. But when he had reached out his hand, she had taken one look at his dirty fingers and screamed her stupid lungs out. It was as if she'd thought he was about to attack her. She had actually cowered against the chauffeur's legs, forcing him to drop the presents that he'd been carrying. At that point Mrs. Ryan had quickly taken charge of the gifts. The chauffeur helped Caitlin safely back into the warm leather comfort of the heated limousine, where no one could touch her.

But all that had happened years ago. Now it was his turn. He would see to it that she paid dearly for the humiliation she had caused him.

They were getting up now, Caitlin and the other girl, preparing to leave the coffee shop. He watched as the four boys with them hovered around Caitlin. He saw the resentful expression on the blond girl's face as she stood slightly to the side of the lively group. Was there jealousy there: jealousy that Caitlin was receiving the attention the other girl thought should be hers? he wondered. Who was she? A friend of Caitlin's? Her roommate? The beginnings of a plan began to form in his mind. Perhaps he could use the blond girl to get close to Caitlin. If she were as jealous as he suspected, he would turn that jealousy to his advantage. Yes, jealousy could be the perfect tool. Julian felt very excited.

But first things first. He had to find a way to meet the blond girl. It should be casual—almost accidental. And once he knew Caitlin's blond friend, once he had gained her confidence, he could put the rest of his plan into action. He would use her to get close to the beautiful Caitlin Ryan—close enough to destroy her.

5

Determined to spend the weekend writing a short essay for her English class, Caitlin went straight back to the dorm after her last class on Friday. Although the paper was not due for another week and a half, she knew she should get it done that weekend because her friend Ginny Brookes was coming the following Saturday. Also, she wanted to have lots of time to write the paper because she knew it had been assigned so the teacher could see how well they wrote.

When she reached her room, she dumped her books on her bed, kicked off her shoes, and, with a huge sigh, plopped down on the remaining space.

"Well, hi, there." Louise turned away from the full-length mirror mounted on the back of her closet door. She had been holding in front of her a turquoise blue cotton sweater. "I was beginning to wonder where you were. You look wiped out."

"I am," Caitlin admitted. "College is a little harder than I thought it would be." Reaching around, she grabbed her pillow, plumped it, and propped it against the headboard. She leaned back on it. Closing her eyes, she said, "Just let me lie here and die for about two minutes. Then, I promise, I'll be more sociable."

"Two minutes?" Louise gave a friendly laugh. "All right. I'll be absolutely silent for two minutes. But then I have to ask you an important question."

"Ummm—okay," Caitlin mumbled.

Now that Caitlin could no longer see her face, Louise relaxed the cheerful look she had affected when Caitlin was looking at her. Almost involuntarily her eyes narrowed as she studied her roommate. Why, she asked herself for the hundredth time since meeting her—did someone like Caitlin Ryan have to come into her life?

And it wasn't just the guys. Girls liked her, too. They flocked to their room to talk or ask Caitlin's opinion about something. And when that happened, Louise felt as if she might as well not be in the room.

Yes, Caitlin was definitely making her feel like old news. The year before, she had been the one everyone had wanted to be with. She had been the girl to be seen with. But now—well, she might as well be invisible.

Oh, how I would love to find some excuse to move out and find another roommate, Louise fumed. But if she did, what good would it do? She'd just be hurting herself. And if she made the sort of snide remarks about Caitlin that she would love to make, she would just be giving everyone an excuse to call her a poor loser.

No. No matter how much it galled her, the only thing to do was to stick to Caitlin like glue, and pretend to be her dearest friend. She would be sure that Caitlin went to all the right parties— such as the mixer that night. That way she would stay popular until the novelty of Caitlin's blue-eyed, black-haired beauty wore off. And it would, Louise was certain of that.

"Your two minutes are up!" she announced. Walking over and sitting down on her own bed, on the side closest to Caitlin, she smiled as Caitlin opened her eyes. "Well, what do you plan to do this weekend, Sleeping Beauty?"

Making a wry face, Caitlin sat up. "I plan to write my first English paper. It isn't due until a week from Monday, but I thought I'd get it over with. By Sunday night I should have it finished."

"By Sunday night *you* should be finished!" Louise commented. "Look at you. What you need is a little R and R: rest and relaxation.

You're right about college being tougher than high school. That's why it's important to take time off to have a little fun once in a while."

"So, what did you have in mind?"

"I thought you'd never ask." Louise grinned. "Remember the mixer is tonight."

"No. I can't go. I already told you that—"

"I know." Louise cut her off with a nod. "Your paper and your letter to Jed. Well, you've already written three this week. What do you want to do, smother the poor guy in an avalanche of paper?"

"All right—then maybe I'll go to a movie," Caitlin replied.

"Don't be ridiculous, Caitlin. No one goes to a movie alone on Friday night." Louise reached out and put her hand on Caitlin's arm. "Listen to me, roomie. You *need* to go to this dance. You *need* to relax." She put her finger to her lips to silence Caitlin when she began to protest again. "It's not like a date. It's just everyone getting together and having fun. Nothing heavy is going to happen."

"I don't know. . . ." Caitlin's voice trailed off. "I really—"

"You should come with me," Louise filled in with a pleading look. "Caitlin, honestly, I don't want to go alone. And I'll have to if you won't come."

"Why don't you go with a boy? There's Josh."

"I told you, it's not that kind of a dance. No

one goes with dates. And that's why it's okay for you to go. Hey, I'll bet even Jed would say you ought to go." Seeing Caitlin began to waver, she leaped up. "Now about that important question I wanted to ask you." Picking up the cotton sweater again, she held it up in front of her. "What do you think? For the mixer, I mean. Is this too bright? I got it at this adorable little boutique in Italy this summer. I didn't have anything particular in mind when I bought it." She shrugged. "I just liked it and figured the perfect place to wear it would come along. Maybe it's right for tonight."

"Oh, it is pretty," Caitlin told her. "It looks great with your coloring." She studied the sweater. "No, I don't think it's too bright."

"Great!" Louise smiled. "Now, what about you?" Tossing the sweater on her bed, she walked to Caitlin's closet and opened the door. She shoved the hangers along the pole and looked through Caitlin's extensive wardrobe. At last she found what she thought was the perfect outfit. Pulling it out, she turned to show Caitlin. "How about this?" It was a bright red straight dress, designed so it would just skim Caitlin's body. Louise turned and glanced into the closet again. "I think this dress would look absolutely wonderful, especially if you add this low slung black belt."

"Louise—"

49

"And how about these to go with it?" Bending down, Louise picked up a pair of black flats with a narrow line of red piping over each toe. "Perfect!"

"I—" Caitlin looked over at Jed's photo, as if to ask what he thought about her going to the dance. "Oh, all right. I'll go." She laughed. "But only because I can't bear the thought of you going alone."

"Oh, great!" Louise grinned. No one would accuse her of being a sore loser.

"But I don't think I want to wear that dress." Pushing herself off the bed, Caitlin walked over and looked past Louise's shoulder into her closet. "I like it, but it's not right." She studied the contents of the jammed closet for a moment, then pulled out a butter yellow cotton knit top with a wide shawl collar. "What do you think? With a pair of black pants?"

"Just a sec." Louise dashed over to her bed, picked up her blue sweater, and came back to stand next to Caitlin. Putting her arm around Caitlin's waist, she turned so they were both looking in the mirror across the room. "Hold your sweater up," she told Caitlin. "There!" She smiled at their reflections. "There's no doubt about it. We will be the most gorgeous girls at the dance."

* * *

Caitlin was having fun. For the first hour of the dance she had felt a guilty pang or two. But then she decided that Louise was right: the mixer was basically a chance for people to meet one another.

Most of the furniture in the largest of the student union lounges had been pushed back in order to provide a place to dance. And there was a band, a really good one.

Caitlin was dancing with the tenth boy who had asked her. The others she had met through Louise or in class. But this boy was someone she had never seen before. He introduced himself as Hal before whirling her onto the floor.

That had been in the middle of a fast dance. The music had been blasting, and there had been no real chance to talk. But then the song had finished, and a slow dance began. Hal had held out his arms, and Caitlin moved into them. She thought that if she didn't, she would have seemed impolite. As soon as possible, though, she set matters straight so he would not get the wrong impression.

"So"—she smiled up at him in a friendly way—"you said you're a prelaw major. My boyfriend is interested in law."

"Your boyfriend?" Hal's eyebrows drew together. "Is he here?" Hal's shaggy blond head swiveled in one direction, then back the other way, as his eyes searched the room. "If he is, then you two must have a pretty open relationship. I've been watching you since you arrived, and you've danced with at least a dozen guys so far."

"Ten," Caitlin corrected, smiling. "And, no, my boyfriend's not here. He's in Montana. He's going to college there for a year."

"Ahhh!" This time the blond eyebrows were raised. "That means I have a chance. When the cat's away—and all that."

"Oh, no." Caitlin laughed. "I don't play."

"You don't!" Hal tried to sound surprised, then drew her closer as the music swirled around them. "Not any kind of games?" he murmured into her ear.

Caitlin could tell by the tone of his voice that Hal was only half-serious. She could hear a touch of humor in his bantering, and she liked him for it. She decided to go along with the game.

"Well—" She hesitated purposefully. "I do play a little tennis, and I like soccer—"

"Tennis!" Hal pushed away from her enough so that he could look directly into her eyes. "Hey, do you really play tennis? I mean halfway decent tennis? How good are you?"

Hal's sudden show of enthusiasm had thrown her off guard. "Uh—well, I was on the team in high school. And I've played in a few country club championships. Does that answer your question?"

"I don't know. How about showing me?"

"I beg your pardon?" It was Caitlin's turn to raise an eyebrow.

"What I mean is, how about a game? Soon. I'm dying to play. My roommate doesn't know a tennis racquet from a Ping-Pong paddle. I've left a note on the bulletin board at the gym, but so far everybody seems too busy to sign up."

"But you've got to give them a chance," Caitlin insisted. "I've been dashing around so much this week that I didn't even notice that there was a bulletin board in the gym."

The slow dance had ended while Caitlin was speaking, but they continued to stand where they were. With a wild strumming on the electric guitar, another fast number began. Hal grabbed her hand and leaned forward, speaking loudly into her ear. "Come on, let's go get some punch. I want to set up a time for us to play."

An hour and a half later Hal and Caitlin were still sitting on the couch where they had taken their cups of punch so they could talk. They had gotten so involved in discussing tennis that it wasn't until the band stopped playing altogether that Caitlin looked up to see that she and Hal were almost the only ones still there. "Oh, wow," she said, checking her watch. "Do you realize what time it is? It's nearly twelve. And if

I'm going to play tennis with you at eight tomorrow morning, I think I'd better get back to the dorm so I can get a little sleep."

"I guess it is late. Sorry, Caitlin. I didn't mean to keep you. Well"—he grinned boyishly— "strike that. Keeping you late was my evil intention when I first saw you and decided to ask you out for coffee after the dance. But now that we're strictly tennis opponents and have a serious match in the morning, I'll walk you home right now."

"Thanks, but"—Caitlin surveyed the nearly empty room—"I came with my roommate. I guess I really should walk home with her."

"If you're talking about the blond girl you came with, I saw her leave about half an hour ago. She was talking to some tall, dark-haired guy. Older looking."

"Ohh! Well, good for her," Caitlin answered, somewhat surprised. The last time she had noticed Louise, she had been dancing with Josh. "In that case, I'll gladly accept your offer. I really don't like the idea of walking across campus at night alone."

"You're right to be cautious," Hal replied. "The buddy system is definitely the best approach." He grinned as he took her arm. "Ready, buddy?"

* * *

After two very close sets of tennis the next morning, Caitlin was ready to admit that she might have met her match. She had played hard but still lost.

"I demand a rematch," she called out to Hal. Laughing and tired, she walked to the bench at the side of the court. Reaching into her sports bag, she pulled out her V-necked white cotton tennis sweater and began to pull it over her head. "You are just too darned good," she told him as he came up to stand beside her.

"Well, you're not so bad yourself," he replied lightly. Picking up a dark green warm-up jacket, he shrugged his arms into it. "If you decide to turn pro, I think Chris and Martina might have some serious competition." The admiration was evident in his warm brown eyes.

"Thanks. I used to think so, too," Caitlin said. She added with a grin, "But, then, how come I couldn't beat you?"

"Hmmm. What if I gave you a chauvinistic answer and said it was because I'm a big, strong guy, and you're only this itty-bitty girl?"

"Oh, I'd probably hit you over the head with this racquet," Caitlin said, pretending to draw back her racquet in a threatening gesture.

"Well, then, I guess I'd better not say that." Hal grinned. "Okay, maybe it's because I had a good day. Or, more likely, it's because you're so good that you cranked up my game a couple of notches. Who knows?" Hal had zipped up his sports bag and set it on the bench. "But I'm all for giving you another chance to beat me. Might I suggest we discuss the details over something cool to drink at the union?"

"Yes, I think I'll take you up on that," Caitlin said, laughing. "*Especially* the part about discussing the details about beating you next time!"

Caitlin and Hal had another game on Thursday afternoon. And that time Caitlin won.

"Okay, now it's my turn to demand a rematch," Hal said, coming up to Caitlin and planting his hands on her shoulders. "What do you say?"

"I say great." She smiled up at him. He was definitely good-looking—and nice. If she weren't so much in love with Jed, Hal was the type of boy she could fall for. But she was just as happy to have him for a friend. And there was no danger their relationship would turn into anything else. Hal understood how she felt about Jed.

"Good. How about Saturday?"

"Sorry." She shook her head. "This weekend's booked. I've got a friend coming from Charlottesville."

"A guy?" Hal gave her a quizzical look.

"Should I be jealous? And, more to the point, should Jed be jealous?"

Caitlin laughed. "*Her* name is Ginny Brookes. She's my best friend from high school. She goes to UVA."

"University of Virginia, huh!" Hal nodded. "Good school. I almost went there." Taking his hands from her shoulders, he walked her off the court. "So Saturday's out. What about next Thursday? In fact, we could set Thursday afternoons as a regular time. We're both free then."

"Good," Caitlin agreed. "Will you reserve a court?"

"Will do." He turned. "Tell me," he inquired, pausing as his lips turned up into a mock wicked smile, "is this girlfriend of yours half as pretty as you are?"

"Hal!" She pretended to protest.

"Hey!" He threw up his hands and backed away a few steps. "If I can't have you, is there any reason why I can't think about moving in on your girlfriend? It's nice being pals with you, but a guy can't exist on friendship alone."

"I'll ask her," Caitlin replied and grinned. "But I honestly don't think you're Ginny's type. She prefers the shy, retiring type."

"Hey!" It was Hal's turn to pretend to hit her with his racquet.

"See you next Thursday," Caitlin promised, blowing him a kiss as she turned to leave.

6

"More coffee?"

Caitlin looked up at the waitress who was hovering over them, then back at her half-filled cup. "Yes, please." Then she glanced at Ginny, as if silently to repeat the waitress's offer.

Ginny glanced down at her cup. "No, thanks. This is just getting cool enough to drink." She smiled at the bone-thin woman in the brown-checked uniform.

After the waitress had refilled Caitlin's cup and left, Caitlin picked up the conversation again. "So, anyway, I told Hal I'd ask you—you know, about maybe going out with him. I mean, now that you're not seeing Bert anymore."

"Oh, wow, thanks a lot." Ginny's tone of mild sarcasm wasn't lost on Caitlin.

"But he's really cute. Honest."

"He just doesn't sound like my type. Or maybe I'm not his type."

Caitlin looked fondly across the table at her

friend, not seeing Ginny's sharp features and rather nondescript, light brown hair, but the real Ginny who was inside—who was so kind and so much fun once her shyness wore off. And she was extremely bright, with a dry wit. "Well, actually, that's exactly what I told Hal—that he probably wasn't your type." She smiled. "You're much too good for him."

"Thanks." Ginny returned a genuine smile. "Anyway, I didn't come up here for a blind date. I came up to see you. And, besides"—a sudden blush tinged her angular cheekbones—"I've already met a guy."

"Oh, really!" Caitlin's eyes lit up with interest. "So, tell me about him," she said, taking a bite of her toast.

When Ginny had arrived at Carleton Hill only an hour before, having driven from Charlottesville, she immediately announced that she was starving. Caitlin had suggested the Hearthside, a coffee shop near campus, known for its good, simple food and English pub atmosphere. She and Ginny were now settled in the deep recesses of a comfortable wooden booth, the remains of their breakfast before them.

"Well, first of all, his name is Winslow Phillips. Everyone calls him Win. And he rides like a demon. I'd almost admit he rides better than I do, but you and I both know that that's impossible." Ginny kept such a straight face that anyone who didn't know her would have thought she was being absolutely serious. Ginny was, in fact, an excellent rider—of almost Olympic caliber. Her goal in life was to manage a horse farm, where she would breed and train the best hunters and jumpers in the country. "He's on a polo team at a club near campus."

"Wow!" Caitlin exclaimed. This guy sounded just right for Ginny.

"Hmmmm." Ginny concentrated, trying to bring Win's face into focus so she could describe him. Then she remembered something. "I don't have to tell you what he looks like. I've got a picture of him. Just a sec." Digging into her purse, which was on the seat beside her, she brought out her wallet and took out a snapshot. "Here." She handed it across the table.

"Um-hmm. I like him," Caitlin said after taking a moment to study the photo. It showed a tall, serious-looking boy dressed in polo attire and holding the reins of a handsome-looking mount. "Is that his horse?" She handed back the photo.

"Yes. One of them. He has four. That's really how we met. I board Cinnamon at the same farm where he keeps his horses."

"How is Cinnamon, by the way?"

"Same as ever—the greatest horse in the world," Ginny boasted with a smile. "You know, that's really why I finally chose the University of Virginia; Charlottesville has some wonderful hunt country. I get a chance to ride almost every day."

"I envy you," Caitlin remarked wistfully. "The horsey set simply doesn't exist here. That's why I decided not to bring Duster. But I do miss him terribly."

"I bet you do!" Ginny shook her head at the thought. "Take Cinnamon away from me and it would be the same as condemning me to a slow death."

"Well, it's not all that bad," Caitlin replied, laughing. "Actually I'm so busy that I probably wouldn't have the time to exercise him as much as I should. So I guess he's better off back at Ryan Acres. I can ride him whenever I go home for a weekend."

"How often do you think you'll be able to get back there?"

Caitln frowned at the question. "Not too often," she admitted. "Not with Colin Wollman there practically day and night. I swear, Ginny"—she shook her head—"it's like this guy has moved in permanently. Fortunately, he does still go home at night."

"Colin?" Ginny's brow furrowed as she tried to think of who Colin Wollman was. "Oh, yeah." She nodded. "I do remember your saying something about him. He's the new lawyer. You think he's really creepy, but I don't remember why."

"He makes my stomach turn over. You know what I mean?" Ginny nodded. "And he's not that new. He took over the legal department at Ryan Mining months ago. The thing is, I can't pinpoint what it is that I don't like about him—I mean the man himself. I definitely do not like the way he's worming his way into my grandmother's and my personal lives." She leaned forward slightly. "Do you know, he's actually in charge of my spending money!"

"No! You're joking."

"I only wish I were. The day before I came up here, he called me into the study and told me how much money *he* was going to allot to me every month."

"But that's horrible."

"You're telling me." An angry look crossed Caitlin's face. "The thing is, I can't really complain to my grandmother, because there's nothing to actually complain about. My so-called 'allowance' is more than generous—probably even more than she would have given me. But it was the way he acted—as if he had every right to take charge. I wanted to tell him off so badly."

"So why didn't you?"

"I don't know, Ginny. I honestly don't know. He came on so nice, saying he remembered what it was like to be in college and how important it was to have enough money to spend and anytime I felt what he was giving me wasn't enough, I should feel free to come and talk to him."

"Well, gosh—" Ginny hesitated. What her friend was telling her didn't seem so horrible. "He doesn't sound so bad."

"It's not the money, it's the principle," Caitlin quickly said, seeing the look of confusion on Ginny's face. "I guess you wouldn't really understand unless you were there. Unless you knew Colin." Angrily, she slumped back against the high wooden seat and scowled. Then, giving herself a strong mental shake, she snapped out of it. "I'm sorry, Ginny. We're supposed to be having fun, not sitting here while I complain about something I can't do anything about. Not now, anyway."

"Does that mean you *do* plan to do something?"

"I don't know. It's too soon to tell, I guess." She wasn't ready to talk to Ginny about her other worries regarding Colin—that she thought something funny was going on between Colin and his sister, Nicole. Or that Nicole and her father were dating. Forcing herself to look cheerful, she said, "Look, enough about Colin Wollman. If you're finished pushing that waffle around your plate, why don't we get out of here. I've been listening to you spout off about how terrific UVA is, now it's my turn. You're going to get the full tour of Carleton Hill, so you can see what you're really missing."

"I have to admit, this is a gorgeous place," Ginny said an hour and a half later as they were heading back to the dorm. She had been shown everything, from the gym, with its indoor tennis courts and Olympic-size pool, to a giant greenhouse filled with rare plants. "I can also see that you've already made several conquests," she said. "Even though you've sworn eternal loyalty to Jed. We must have passed a dozen guys who yelled hi or stopped to talk to you."

Caitlin laughed. "You're exaggerating. It was only a few. And they're just friends. Is there anything wrong with having friends who also happen to be boys?"

"Did I even *hint* that there was anything wrong with it?" Ginny's eyes twinkled. "I was just making a comment."

Suddenly Caitlin stopped and grabbed her friend's arm impulsively. "Oh, Ginny! I really have missed you. I wish you were going here— and that we were roommates again."

"I miss you, too, Caitlin." A tiny frown line creased her forehead. "Is there something wrong? Something you haven't told me about?

How about your roommate? You haven't told me much about her. Do you like her?"

"Louise!" Caitlin shook her head. "Oh, sure—sure I do. Louise is nice. She's pretty—and very popular. I haven't seen very much of her this past week, since she met some guy. A senior. He's premed, I think. She's been out with him almost every night." Caitlin shrugged and gave a little laugh. "I guess that's what it really is. I'm lonely. Dorm rooms can seem so empty when you're by yourself." She smiled at Ginny. "I miss not having you to talk to, and I miss everyone from Highgate. You, Jed—"

"Well, but Matt Jenks is here, isn't he?"

"He is. I saw him at orientation week, and I ran into him in the bookstore the first week. But we didn't get a chance to talk for very long that time. He was late to some class." Caitlin looked thoughtful. "Come to think of it, he was acting almost as though he didn't *want* to talk to me."

"That's a little weird!" Ginny commented softly.

"I know," Caitlin agreed, then added, "Oh, listen, I'm probably reading something into it that isn't there. After all, he did say he'd decided to change his major to premed. That means he'll have to completely rearrange his schedule. I don't know if they'll let him do it this semester. But maybe, since it's so early in the year. That must be it."

"I can understand that," Ginny said. "It's tough enough getting used to one class schedule. If I had to change mine, I'd go crazy." Dismissing Matt from her mind, she suddenly clapped her hands together. "Hey! Didn't you just say you were lonely? Well, here I am! Take advantage. Let's talk up a storm." She linked her arm with Caitlin's. "And it only took me two hours to drive here from Charlottesville, so it's not as though we're a continent apart or anything." Then she added, "Just don't expect me to come up on any of the weekends when there's a polo match going on."

"Fair enough!" Caitlin smiled. "And maybe some weekend, when there is a match, I can drive down and we can both watch Win play. We could even have a tailgate party."

"That's a great idea. I brought my picnic basket with me to school. You know, that big wicker hamper we used to use to pack hunt breakfasts in? And there's this great deli near campus that makes up the most incredible picnic lunches."

"That sounds like so much fun. Find out when Win's going to play and let me know. Okay?"

They were passing the Omega Psi house. Several of the fraternity members were hanging out on the porch, lounging on the railing and the steps. One of them waved and called, "Hey,

Caitlin! Hello! What's the matter, are you too stuck up to say hi?"

Caitlin turned and, recognizing Darrell Hart as the boy who'd called her name, raised her arm and waved back. "Hi, there, Darrell. I didn't see you. Sorry."

"Well, I guess I'll forgive you, then," Darrell called back.

"He'd forgive anyone as pretty as you," another guy called, then ducked as Darrell playfully took a swing at him.

"More friends?" Ginny said teasingly as they walked on.

"Actually, he's Louise's friend."

"Hmm. Looks to me as though he'd rather be yours."

"Honestly, Ginny!" Caitlin protested. "You know that Jed's the only one for me. But I can't become a hermit." She found herself repeating Louise's warning.

"Well, I won't argue with you there!" Ginny said. Suddenly, she pointed at a large, two-story, yellow brick house on the other side of the street. "Oh, look! You have a branch of Alpha Phi here."

"Are you planning to pledge at UVA?" Caitlin asked.

"Um-hmm. Both my aunt and my mother were Alpha Phis, so I'm pretty much set to pledge there. For me, rush week will just be a formality. How about you? Have you thought about which house you want to pledge?"

"I'm not sure I'm even going to join a sorority," Caitlin replied. "My roommate didn't join last year. And she's hardly what you'd call a social outcast." Caitlin regarded Ginny. "I can't believe that *you're* joining a sorority. You hated doing things in groups at Highgate."

"You're right," Ginny admitted. "If my aunt and mother hadn't talked it up so much, I might not have been interested. But I thought about it. It's a great way to make friends and eventually I'll be able to live in the sorority house. It's a lot better than living in a dorm and existing on cafeteria food!"

"You're right about that," Caitlin said. "Maybe I will join. I'd rather live in a house than in the dorm, too. Maybe I'll even see if I can talk Louise into joining."

"A sophomore? I don't know. All the good houses will probably have their quota filled with freshmen."

"Maybe, maybe not. Anyway, as I said, I haven't made up my mind yet."

"Well, you'd better decide. When is rush week here, anyway?"

"Formal rushing starts the week after next."

"Then you'd really better start doing some thinking—fast!" Ginny said.

Caitlin nodded slowly. "Yes, I guess I'd better."

7

"Mail call!" Louise said cheerfully as she came into the room on Friday afternoon at the end of rush week.

"Oh, great!" Caitlin looked up from where she was curled up on her bed, studying for an art history test. Louise had her arms piled high with envelopes, magazines, and a small package. Caitlin hoped that one of those envelopes would be from Jed. It had been almost two weeks since she had heard from him, and she was beginning to worry.

"The package is for me," Louise said, tossing it on her bed. She walked over to Caitlin. "The *Vogue* and the *Town and Country* are for you." She handed them to her. "Here's a letter from your grandmother—on that luscious gray stationery that I adore. And here's one from Ryan Mining— very official looking. A bill from that boutique in town. And this"—she held the envelope up to the light—"looks like a card from that friend of

69

yours at UVA." Drawing her eyebrows together, she looked at Caitlin. "Is it your birthday? How come you didn't tell me?"

"No, it's not until November," Caitlin replied. "Ginny's terrible about dates, so she always gets me a card early. That way she figures she'll never be late." Suddenly Caitlin felt very impatient. "Come on, Louise, what else is there?"

"Well, if you're wondering if there's a letter from Jed, there isn't. Sorry," Louise commiserated. "I would have given it to you right away. And here's the rest." She tossed three more envelopes down on the bed. Lousie stared down at Caitlin and folded her arms. "It's been a couple of weeks since you've gotten a letter, hasn't it?"

"Yes." Caitlin smiled weakly. "It's not that I'm worried. He's probably had a lot of studying to do," she said, making excuses for Jed. "In fact, I think he did mention something about having to do a paper in animal husbandry that was going to keep him busy for a while."

"Uh-huh. Well, all I know is that you've been up to your eyeballs in rush activities, plus your studies. But you still managed to find time to write to him." Louise walked to her desk to put down her mail. "Maybe I shouldn't say this, Caitlin, but aren't you starting to get a little worried?" Dropping her envelopes on the desk, she turned and leaned against it, folding her arms. "I mean—you know, it's the guy who usually bails out of a long-distance relationship first. They're just weaker, that's all."

"Jed is not weak!" Caitlin objected. She picked up the first letter on the pile but did not open it.

"If you say so." Louise tossed her head impatiently, causing a lock of silken hair to fall over one eye. She reached up and pushed it back. "It's just that I think you should be dating other guys. There are certainly tons of guys who want to ask you out. And they're *here*," she said with emphasis, "not two thousand miles away where you can't keep an eye on them."

As she got in the last dig, Louise managed to keep a sympathetic expression on her face. Inside, though, she was gloating. Caitlin was definitely suffering, and she—Louise—was loving every minute of it. She watched as Caitlin stared off in the distance and began absent-mindedly toying with the letter. Things were turning out just as Julian had said they would. Caitlin was becoming unsure of Jed's feelings for her, and soon enough she'd start feeling unsure of herself in other areas. And with her self-confidence shattered, her popularity would disappear, too.

Julian. Kind, thoughtful, understanding Julian. *What would I do without him*? Louise wondered. He knew so much. He seemed so much older and wiser than the other guys she knew.

When he had first suggested they destroy Caitlin's relationship with Jed, Louise had argued that it would just make Caitlin free to date again. And Louise certainly didn't need any more competition. But Julian had promised her that Caitlin would be so devastated by Jed's rejection of her that she would retreat into herself. And no one would want to be around her, girls or guys.

Oh, she was so glad she had confided in Julian about her problems with Caitlin. At first she hadn't been sure if she should or not. But after she had known Julian for a while, his kindness and sensitivity won her over. One night she had finally told him what a pain she thought Caitlin was—about how snobby and unappreciative she could be. After everything she had done to make Caitlin feel welcome—introducing her to her friends, making sure she was never left out— Louise hadn't received one word of thanks. And what angered Louise the most was the fact that now Caitlin seemed to think she was Miss Popularity.

After listening to everything she had to say, Julian had calmed her down. Then, in his wonderfully soothing voice, he had told her how they could knock Caitlin down a peg or two.

It wasn't, Louise argued with herself, that she wanted to destroy Caitlin. She wanted Caitlin to understand, to feel what she was feeling—to know what it was to lose something that was important to her. It didn't matter if it was one boy's love or the admiration of most of the boys on campus.

Caitlin still had that faraway look in her eyes. Louise thought it was time she said something to snap her out of her trance.

"Oh, Caitlin, forget what I said. I should have kept my mouth shut. You're absolutely right— Jed's probably working on some huge project that's taking up all of his time. You'll probably get a letter tomorrow. Stop looking so sad, okay?"

"Hmmm—what?" Caitlin stared at Louise, only hearing part of what she'd said. "I'm sorry," she apologized. "I was just thinking . . ." She allowed her sentence to drop. "What did you say?"

"I was telling you to stop worrying. You're bound to get a letter from Jed soon." She smiled. "And I wanted to remind you that you said you'd go for a hamburger at the Hearthside with Julian and me. You know he's dying to meet you."

"I'm looking forward to meeting him, too," Caitlin said. "He sounds terrific."

"Not to mention good-looking," Louise added.

"Oh, of course!" Caitlin laughed. "Tall, dark,

and mysteriously handsome. That's how you first described him, remember?"

"And it's true." Louise glanced down at her watch. "He'll be here to pick us up in about two hours, at five-thirty." She turned to pick up her purse from the top of the desk. "But I've got to run an errand first. I'll tell you what—why don't you go down to the lobby about then, and I'll meet you both there. Okay? I don't think I'll be late, but in case I am, I hate to think of him sitting down there by himself."

"Sure," Caitlin promised. She winked. "And I'll know him the minute I see him—tall, dark, and—"

"Mysteriously handsome!" the two girls finished in unison. Then they both laughed.

But as soon as Louise left, Caitlin's face took on a troubled, unhappy expression. Listlessly, she picked up the envelopes Louise had dropped on her bed and began to leaf through them.

She opened her grandmother's letter first, skimming through it in a matter of seconds. It was the usual weekly letter, written as impersonally as if Regina Ryan were composing an annual report for the board of directors of Ryan Mining. She was thinking of draining the swimming pool. Duster was getting plenty of exercise and looking fit. Rollins had a cold, and so one of the maids had to take over his indoor duties. She and Colin had gone to Washington to see a new musical. . . . Caitlin stuffed the letter back into its expensive envelope, with the estate address engraved in black on the back flap. "Enough is enough," she muttered as she put down the envelope and picked up the next one.

It was the letter Louise had called "official looking," the one from Ryan Mining headquarters. She knew what it was: her allowance from Colin. She ripped it open and glanced at the check inside. Yes, it was generous. More than she really needed, in fact. She tossed the envelope down on the end of the bed. She didn't bother opening the bill from the boutique, which was supposed to have gone directly to Colin. He was handling all her bills now, too. She would call the boutique in the morning and inform them, but she didn't feel like doing it right then.

Finally, she picked up the card from Ginny. For the first time since Louise had come into the room with the mail, Caitlin felt like smiling a little. Ginny always had a way of picking out just the right card. She savored each moment that it took to slit open the envelope, lift the flap, and pull out the card.

It was a fold-out card. Two horses, touching noses, were on the front. One looked remarkably like Duster, the other a little like Ginny's horse, Cinnamon. Above their heads was printed the single word "Hay!" She unfolded the card. It stretched out to show that the horse that looked like Cinnamon was actually in a trailer, way down a road. Inside, the printing continued. "We may be far apart, but that doesn't mean we can't still be close friends. Happy Birthday!"

A tear welled up in the corner of Caitlin's eye. It slid down her cheek as she rose and walked to the desk, carrying the card with her. She propped it up where she could look at it. She decided to write to Ginny immediately.

But before she opened the top drawer to take out her stationery, her glance fell on the photo of Jed on her dresser and lingered there. Oh, how she longed to reach out and run her finger along his cheek down to the cleft in his chin, to touch, ever so lightly, the corner of his lips as he smiled his lopsided smile, to run her fingers—Well, all right, she would write him first. But not one word, she promised herself, not one single line about how long it had been since she had received a letter from him.

With all good intentions firm in her mind, she picked up her box of stationery and carried it back to the bed. There she curled up against the pillows and took out a sheet of light blue paper. Bracing the box against her knees to make a desk, she began to write:

Dearest Jed,
     How I miss you. I hate it when you don't write. Is something wrong? You know—

She crumpled up the sheet of paper and tossed it onto the floor beside the bed.

Dear Jed,
     It's been almost two weeks since I received a letter from you. Why haven't—

This time she gave a heavy sigh as she wadded the paper up into a ball. That wouldn't do at all. The letter should be cheerful, light-hearted—nothing heavy. She tapped her chin with the end of her pen, thinking. Actually there was a lot she could write about. It had been a busy week. And the two letters she had written a couple of days before had really only been short notes. Pulling out a fresh sheet, she started once again.

Dear Jed,
     Well, rush week is finally over. I don't know whether to be relieved or sad. It was a lot of fun, but also terribly exhausting. First there were the "open house" parties. Everyone who has registered for rush week is expected to attend each party. There are nine houses on campus, and by the time I got to about the seventh, I was so full of tea I felt like a sponge. Then came the "invitation-only" parties. You don't have to go to

every one you're invited to—only the houses you're really interested in joining. That really narrowed it down for me. Those parties were fun, with skits and singing, and I got to meet a lot of girls I wouldn't ordinarily get to meet because they're older.

I guess I shouldn't keep you in suspense any longer and tell you which sorority I'm planning to pledge. Are you in suspense, Jed? I wonder. Knowing that at your college there aren't any sororities or fraternities, I suppose you've got other things on your mind.

There, she thought, maybe that would prompt him to explain why he hadn't written to her for so long.

I've decided to pledge Kappa Kappa Delta. It's not a national sorority, but it's the one I like best. Their charity is the Disabled Children's Foundation; and you know how much I care about disabled kids.

For a moment her mind flew back to little Ian Foster, the child who had become temporarily crippled because of her carelessness. It had been a dark time in her life, but she had learned to live with the memory. And she felt that she was a stronger person for it.

Louise, my roommate, is pledging Kappa Kappa Delta, too. We were "pearled" last night. That was the highlight of rush week. I'm sure you don't know what that means, so I'll explain.

At the last party at the house you've decided you want to join, an "active" member of the sorority whom you've become closest to puts a string of pearls around your neck. While she does it, she tells you what being a member of that sorority means to her. Carol, the girl who pearled me, was so sweet. It was all so moving that we both ended up crying. But, then, so did just about every other girl who was being pearled. And now we're supposed to wear our pearls all the time. It's not mandatory, or anything like that. It's more of a tradition. But I like it. Now I feel like a true sorority sister—even though I'll only be a pledge and not an active until initiation next spring. Some girls even wear their pearls to bed, but I'm not going that far. Still, you'll probably see me wearing them when you come for Christmas. (Just a tiny reminder, Jed.)

Tonight's the final party of rush week. It's called the "preference party," because the sorority we go to is the one we'll join. It's supposed to be very formal and very serious. I'm a little nervous, and Louise is, too. So we're going out early, with a friend of hers, to have hamburgers. That way we won't have to eat just before the party. I'd better end this letter so I'll have time to take it right to the campus post office.

I'll think about it flying out to you, and all the time I'll wish I could be coming with it. Oh, Jed, I love you so very, very much. I just keep thinking what a long time it is until Christmas. Take care of yourself.

Love,
Caitlin

Caitlin read the letter over and, satisfied, folded it and slipped it into an envelope. After addressing it, she kissed it for good luck. She glanced at her watch again. If she hurried, she'd have just enough time to walk to the post office and get back before Louise's friend Julian got there.

8

Caitlin decided to change her clothes before she went to the post office to mail Jed's letter. If she did that, she would be ready to go to the Hearthside as soon as Louise returned and her friend Julian arrived. Checking through her closet, she settled on a pair of classic pleated slacks and an oversize periwinkle-blue sweater with a cowl neck. After brushing out her dark hair, she added a touch of gloss to her lips.

She picked up Jed's letter, put a stamp on it, and stuffed it into her purse. In case Louise returned before she did, she went to Louise's desk and scribbled a quick note saying that she would be back in a few minutes.

It was a lovely late afternoon. Although it was warm and the leaves were still on the trees, Caitlin could sense that fall would soon arrive. The sky was a true cobalt blue, making the lawns and flowers stand out in vivid contrast. Oh, if only Jed were here, she thought, breathing in the first chill air, they could stroll along holding hands, talking—

Her thoughts were interrupted by the soft thudding of someone jogging by. She started to move off the path to allow whoever it was to pass, when he came up beside her and started to jog in place. She turned to see Hal, dressed in a burgundy sweat suit, his face flushed from his run. "Hi," he said breathlessly. "Where're you heading?"

"The post office." She smiled. "Don't let me keep you."

"Actually, you're giving me a chance to slow down for a minute." He paused to take a ragged breath. "I need to." He took another breath. "I think I'm a little out of shape because I didn't get to play tennis with you this week. But I guess you've been in and out of a few sororities this week."

"You said it," she agreed. "I gather you're pledging, too?"

"Yeah—Omega Psi."

"Great! Isn't that Darrell Hart's fraternity?"

"Right." Hal looked surprised. "You know him?"

"I met him through my roommate, Louise," she explained. "They went out last year."

"Ah." Hal raised an arm to blot some of the perspiration from his forehead. "Listen, back to tennis. Are we on for this Thursday?"

82

"You'd better believe it. I think I'm going to need some exercise, considering all the parties I've been to this past week. I must have gained five pounds."

"Hmmm." Hal looked appreciatively at her. "You look pretty good to me!"

"Hal, honestly. How can you tell?" Caitlin laughed. "I've got on a large sweater."

"Didn't you know?" Hal said, raising his blond eyebrows. "Under this nondescript sweatshirt lies my greatest secret—my red, yellow, and blue Superman outfit." He thumped his chest. "I've got X-ray vision. And now I guess I'd better be 'up, up, and away,' before my true identity is revealed." He grinned and gave her a snappy little salute. "See you Thursday, if not before. And remember, don't tell anyone who I really am."

"I wouldn't dream of it," she called out, laughing. She stood, watching him jog away for a second, then turned. A few minutes later she was climbing the steps to the college branch of the post office.

She was just about to open the little door of the out-of-town mail slot, when a hand reached past her shoulder and opened it for her.

"Thanks," she told the unseen person behind her as she dropped Jed's letter in. Turning around, she saw who it was. "Matt, hi there!" She smiled at the handsome boy who had been her friend at Highgate Academy, as well as Jed's roommate. "How are you? I haven't seen you since the first week of school at the bookstore." She gave a quick glance over her shoulder at the mailbox. "That was a letter to Jed I was just mailing."

"Hi, yourself!" Matt grinned. "I know. I saw the address on the envelope. And yeah, I wondered why I hadn't seen you around. I keep thinking we're going to run into each other. I guess we're like ships in the night."

"Ships?"

"You know, like the old saying—passing, but not seeing each other. I guess it's a bigger campus than we think." He pushed open the outer door, and they walked down the steps together. "About that letter to Jed—I just mailed one myself in answer to his that I got yesterday."

"Yesterday!" Caitlin felt slightly stunned at Matt's news. How could Jed have had time to write to Matt, and not to her? She felt as though she'd been kicked in the stomach. Not wanting Matt to see her reaction, however, she covered it with a smile. Trying to sound casual, she said, "So you got a letter yesterday?"

"Uh-huh." They had reached the bottom of the steps. "He sounds like he's really getting into his classes. He spent most of the letter telling me how he and his friend Eve are working together on a project in range-management class. The class must be really tough, though. It sounded like they're putting in a lot of time on the project, even nights."

"Eve?"

"Yeah." Matt nodded, noticing for the first time how pale Caitlin had become. "Hey, Caitlin!" Matt's voice showed concern. "Are you all right? You look kind of funny."

"Me?" She forced a smile. "No, I'm fine!" Caitlin was struggling to remain cool; the last thing she wanted was for Matt to guess how she really felt. But what she really wanted to do was grab him by the collar and demand to know everything he could tell her about what was going on between Jed and Eve. Why hadn't Jed mentioned that Eve was at Montana Agricultural, too? Her mind reeled. What had Matt said—that they'd been spending *nights* together? Nights when Jed could have been writing to her—

"Are you sure you're okay?" Matt's hand was on her shoulder, and he looked concerned. "I didn't—"

"Matt, I'm fine. Honestly!" Caitlin felt a tiny muscle at the corner of her mouth begin to quiver. She raised a hand to cover it. "Look, Matt, it was really wonderful running into you." She glanced at her watch. "But I've got to run. I'm meeting someone. And—I'm a little late."

"Right." Matt looked slightly confused. "Hey, let's try to get together sometime," he said as she was turning and starting to hurry away. "Maybe next week!"

But Caitlin didn't answer. She already had her face bent down in the cowl collar of her sweater. Tears were beginning to roll down her cheeks.

Eve—Eve—Eve, the name kept repeating itself over and over in her mind as she stumbled down the brick walkway.

Oh, how could Jed do this to her? Why hadn't he told her that Eve was at Montana Agricultural College with him? And how could he even talk to that horrible girl again—after what she had done a few short months before? Caitlin nearly was killed because of a lousy stunt Eve had rigged.

Eve had had it in for Caitlin from the minute Caitlin had arrived in Montana to spend a month with Jed on his father's ranch. She had continually done her best to convince everyone, including Caitlin, that Caitlin didn't belong there. And her final, nearly fatal, trick had been to slit the cinch of Caitlin's saddle before the big race at the fair, so that it would fall off during the race, leaving Eve to win. Fortunately, the cinch had given way at the start of the race. And with her quick reflexes, Caitlin had managed to leap free of the startled, plunging horse.

If she hadn't, she could easily have been

trampled beneath the horse's powerful hooves. As it was, she had proved what an excellent horsewoman she was by controlling the frightened animal and then leaping onto his bare back to win the race. In doing so, she not only beat Eve but also proved herself and won the admiration of Jed's sister and his friends.

Caitlin remembered how she had later confronted Eve, warning her not to try to pull any more tricks.

Was Eve still challenging her? Even from two thousand miles away? A vision of Eve's pretty face swam before Caitlin's eyes. It was as if the girl with the mass of taffy-colored hair and the turquoise eyes was laughing at her, taunting Caitlin and saying she might as well forget Jed. It was as though she were telling Caitlin that she had won after all. Jed was hers now. And Caitlin was two thousand lonely miles away from him—*away from him—away from him.*

Caitlin shook her head to rid herself of the vision of Eve. Suddenly she realized she was standing in front of her dorm. She had walked all the way across campus, yet she could not recall having taken a single step since she had left Matt at the post office. Reaching up, she wiped away the last of her tears. Her eyes burned as though she hadn't slept for a few days. And there was an actual physical pain at the back of her throat.

A girl came down the steps, calling out hello to Caitlin as she passed. Caitlin did not respond. Slowly she began to mount the steps. As she did, she walked into the lobby and started toward the back, where the elevators were located. It was then that she met Julian Stokes for the first time—or for what she thought was the first time.

9

Julian spotted Caitlin as soon as she had entered
the lobby. How could he not? Her radiant beauty
lit up even the darkest room. To him, she would
always be the most beautiful girl in the world.
That was what he had thought ever since she
was seven and he was ten. She was also the
person he hated more than he could imagine
hating anyone. His need for revenge for the
humiliation he had endured at her hands took
second place only to his burning desire to
become a doctor.

As he rose to greet her, he reminded himself
that he was no longer the ragged little boy in the
mining town. He was now a brilliant premed
student—the head of his class. That meant that
he was well on his way to becoming a wealthy
and successful doctor. As far as he was concerned, he was now on equal footing with Caitlin Ryan.

But why, then, with all his self-assurance, was

he feeling as though a bolt of lightning had just struck him?

"Hello!" Julian put every ounce of charm he could summon into that one word. "I'm Julian Stokes." He held out his hand for her to shake.

She didn't say anything. She just stood there, looking at him. No, it was more as if she were looking *through* him.

"You're Caitlin Ryan, of course. Louise has told me so much about you. I couldn't help recognizing you. I'm glad you're joining us at the Hearthside." He paused. She still had not taken his hand. *Why not, for God's sake?* It was stuck out there, in midair. But he couldn't just let it drop, could he? That would be a sign of defeat. He decided to smile at her. Girls were always telling him what an irresistible smile he had. He looked deeply into her eyes and smiled.

Finally she spoke. But it was in a voice that left no doubt as to how she felt—she didn't really consider him important enough even to talk to. "I'm terribly sorry, I—I don't feel hungry. If you'll excuse me, I have to go up to my room."

Stunned, Julian could only stand and watch her walk away from him. Finally, he lowered his arm, clenching his hand into a fist, then straightening it out, then clenching it again. For almost eleven years he had waited for this moment. Eleven years of thinking and planning and dreaming. He had worked hard, dedicating himself to his studies. He had come this far completely on his own. No one had helped; no one had even encouraged him. His father, who was now coughing out the pitiful remainder of his life with black lung disease, had bitterly told Julian he was stupid if he thought he could ever be anything but a miner. But he hadn't listened. Finally Julian had managed to win a full scholarship to Carleton Hill, one of the most prestigious colleges in the country. Not only that, but he had distinguished himself at the research lab where he worked to earn his spending money while still maintaining an honors grade average. And in a year he'd be starting his medical training. He was confident he would be accepted to any school to which he applied.

And yet, nothing had really changed at all. Caitlin Ryan still thought of herself as a princess—and of him as an insignificant commoner.

Julian wanted to walk. He needed to walk. It didn't matter where he went—as long as he kept moving. He needed to release some of his anger before he did something he might later regret.

He turned and strode from the lobby, slamming the door behind him. As he dashed down the steps three at a time, the open front of his raincoat flew out on either side of him, like the wings of a great dark bird.

* * *

Louise returned from her errand. As she entered the lobby, she looked for Julian, expecting to see him waiting there with Caitlin. When she saw neither of them, she went immediately to the elevator and took it to the third floor, where their room was located.

"Caitlin"—she called her roommate's name before she was halfway into the room—"what are you doing up here? Did Julian call and say he was going to be late? What happened?"

Caitlin looked up at Louise from where she lay, stomach down, on her bed. "Isn't he downstairs? That's where I left him."

"You left him!" Louise's voice was close to a shout. She lowered her voice. "No, he's not downstairs. And what do you mean, that's where you left him? Why didn't you stay down there with him? I told you I might be a little late. You were supposed to keep him company until I got back."

Then, for the first time since she had entered the room, she took a good look at Caitlin. She bent closer. Something was wrong. Caitlin's eyes were red and swollen. "Hey!" she said, softening her voice. She sat down on the edge of the bed and gently put her hand on Caitlin's shoulder. "What's wrong?"

"Nothing," Caitlin said vaguely. "I'm fine, really." She pulled herself up and turned around, her knees to one side. "I must have

fallen asleep," she lied. "When I came back from
the post office, I suddenly realized how tired I
was, so I decided it would be better to take a nap
than go with you two. I'd really be a drag. I hope
you don't mind. I apologized to your friend."
She looked at Louise. "Isn't he down in the
lobby?"

"No, he's not." Louise stared at Caitlin, totally
unconvinced by what Caitlin had said. She
wasn't just tired. Something had happened. She
had never seen Caitlin act this way before. What
had Julian said to her? "Caitlin"—her voice was
cautious—"did Julian say something to upset
you?"

It was Caitlin's turn to stare. "No, of course
not!" She shook her head. "Look, it's just as I
said. The fresh air and the walk got to me,
somehow. By the time I reached the lobby, I was
sleepy. I apologized to him and came right up
here."

"Okay. Okay." Caitlin was sticking to her
story, but Louise didn't believe it. Caitlin wasn't
the type of person who took naps during the
day. If anyone was a bundle of boundless
energy, Louise thought, it was dear little Caitlin.
"I think I'd better go find him to exlain why I
was late. I'm afraid he might be angry." She
glanced briefly at her watch. Then, frowning,
she looked at it again. "But I'm not late! I
wonder—" She started for the door, then

stopped and looked back. "I'll be back in plenty of time to get ready for the party. So don't worry."

"The party!" Caitlin leaped to her feet. "Oh, my gosh! I forgot all about the party. I don't believe it." She looked around frantically, still feeling somewhat disoriented. How long had it been since she'd walked to the post office? It seemed like hours. Yet—she glanced out of the window—it wasn't even dark yet. "What time did you say it was?" Her heart was beating fast.

"Caitlin! Calm down!" Louise came back to where her roommate was standing and put both hands on her shoulders. "It's only five-thirty, and you've got plenty of time to get dressed. In fact, if I find Julian, I'm going to see if he'll still go out with me for a hamburger. And I'll bring one back for you. Meanwhile, why don't you just take a long shower and relax. Okay?"

Caitlin nodded numbly. After Louise left, Caitlin sat back down on the edge of the bed. Her heart was beginning to slow down to its normal rhythm again, and her mind was starting to clear. Louise was right. There was plenty of time. And she needed it. She needed time to think.

An hour later, Louise finally found Julian. She had looked everywhere—the library, the union, even at his small apartment three blocks from campus. It wasn't until then that it dawned on her where he must be.

She saw him as soon as she walked into the Hearthside—in a booth in the back, a cup of coffee in front of him. He was stirring it absently as she slid into the seat opposite him.

"Hi, Julian!" She smiled at him, even though he didn't bother to look up. "Why didn't you wait for me at the dorm? I wasn't late." She hesitated. "Julian?"

He raised his head. His dark brows were drawn tightly together in a scowl, his slate-colored eyes clouded and brooding. "Because I didn't feel like sitting in the lobby of a girls' dorm any longer. I knew you'd come here eventually."

"Oh, did you!" Louise felt a little miffed. "Did you really, Julian!" She knew she sounded like a shrew, but she could help it. He was taking her for granted.

"Yes." Julian's voice was a growl. "I did. After all, you're not stupid, Louise. And this hick town isn't that big."

"Oh!" Louise replied in a small voice. Her brow furrowed slightly. She hated it when Julian got in one of his black moods. She never understood him then.

What was wrong with everyone today, anyway? she wondered. *Is it because this is the end of pledge week? But—oh, that's a stupid way to think,* she told herself. Julian didn't have anything to do with pledge week. He didn't even belong to a fraternity. She almost giggled. Julian had his own little fraternity—all those groupies who considered him to be some kind of guru because he had an answer for everything. But, then, that was exactly why she was spending so much time with him—because he understood her, because he wanted to help her deal with Caitlin.

"Did you want something?" Julian's question broke into her musings.

"What?" She looked at him, focusing her eyes. "Did you just ask if I wanted something?" She caught a movement in the corner of her eye and glanced to see what it was. The waitress was standing there. "Oh!" She looked back at him. "Are you having something?"

"Just coffee."

"Then just coffee for me, too." Remembering her promise to Caitlin, she added, "And I'd also like a hamburger to go, please. No onions."

As soon as the waitress left to take care of Louise's order, Julian said, "I've been doing some thinking. About Caitlin."

"Oh?"

"Yes. I met her at the dorm before I left. And now I really understand how you feel about her."

"Really?" She felt her eyes widen. Was he going to tell her something juicy about Caitlin—

about something she had said to him? Maybe what he was about to say would explain why Caitlin was acting so weirdly. She leaned forward. "What happened?"

"Happened? What makes you think something happened?"

Julian was glaring at her in a way that made her feel suddenly stupid and awkward. "Well—I just thought—" she stammered.

"Louise, that's your problem, you think too much." All at once Julian smiled. "Why don't you let me do the thinking." His voice was soothing. Reaching across that table, he covered her hand lightly with his own. "Just do what I tell you, and everything will turn out just fine."

Louise nodded, mesmerized.

"I've come across some very useful information. There's a Matt Jenks, a freshman, who's just joined my study group. I'm helping him in physiology. Apparently he's friends with Caitlin's boyfriend, Jed—as well as with Caitlin herself. Anyway, I was asking him some questions about them. And Matt told me about a girl named Eve who Jed is working with on a class project in Montana. This Eve is spending a lot of time with Caitlin's precious Jed, and Matt said Jed used to go out with her."

He paused as the waitress returned with Louise's coffee. As soon as she had gone, he resumed. "What I think we should do is make

Caitlin doubt Jed's loyalty to her. You could say that you heard, from me, that Jed's spending a lot more time with Eve than he needs to if they're just studying together."

"But I don't understand. How could it be believable that this information came from you?" Louise asked. She was having a terrible time following all of this.

Julian smiled patiently at her. "All you have to say is that Matt approached me to ask if he should tell Caitlin about what was happening between Jed and Eve. Then you say that I advised him not to become involved. But, I did tell you because I thought you might be concerned about Caitlin, since she's your roommate. Now do you understand?"

"I think so." Louise nodded, even though she wasn't all that sure. "But what if she confronts this Matt and demands to know why he didn't level with her?"

"You'll simply have to convince her that that wouldn't be smart."

"All right. I guess I can do that." Louise flashed him a smile. She wanted to show Julian that she could be as devious as he was. "In fact," she said, "I've already got her worrying about how hard it is to keep a long-distance relationship, as you suggested."

"Just one word of caution, though, Louise. Don't move too quickly. It will look suspicious.

She'll start wondering why you're pushing so hard. Just be kind and sweet, and make her feel as if you have her best interests at heart. Then, when she's firmly convinced that Jed is dating his former girlfriend again, I'll step in." He didn't bother to tell her what he had planned next—that splitting up Jed and Caitlin was only the beginning of his plan to have his revenge. There was really no need. If Louise did her part as well as he hoped she would, he might not have to tell her anything more. Well, he would see.

"Julian?" Louise was hesitant. But there was a question she had to ask, and it couldn't wait any longer. "Why are you helping me get back at Caitlin? I mean, you don't even really know her."

"I just told you why," he replied. "I think you're right about her, and someone needs to teach her a lesson." Then he reached up to gently touch her face. "Besides, I care about you, and if she's hurting you, it hurts me, too."

Louise continued to study him. It was a nice speech, but she didn't believe it for a minute. She also knew there was no point in pursuing the argument. Eventually she would discover his reasons.

The waitress returned, this time with the hamburger for Caitlin. She placed the wrapped burger on the table, along with Louise's check.

99

"Well, I guess I'd better go." Louise picked up the food and the check and started to rise.

"Here, let me get that." Julian reached for the check.

"Well, you can get the coffee. But the hamburger is for Caitlin. I think I should pay for that."

"Come on, Louise," Julian said as he took the check from her. "Considering what we have planned for Caitlin, the least I can do is buy her a hamburger. Don't you think?"

10

It was still raining. Caitlin could hear the drops on the windowpanes, even though the covers were pulled up over her head. The rain had started the night before, just as they were coming home from the party at the Kappa Kappa Delta house. She, Louise, and two other girls had had to make a dash for the front door of the dorm, their coats held over their heads to keep them from being drenched.

By the time they had made it inside, Caitlin's silk dress was one huge water stain. But it was worth it. The party had been even more fun that she had dreamed: laughter and skits, then candlelight and songs and sentimental tears. How could she ever have toyed with the idea of not joining a sorority? She could hardly wait to tell Jed about it.

Jed! Her eyes flew open.

Jed and Eve!

Eve and Jed!

Caitlin thought back through the events of the afternoon before. Back to when Matt had told her about Eve. Eve was actually at the same school with Jed. Caitlin finally decided that she had allowed her imagination to conjure up the worst possible scenario. After all, if Jed really were seeing Eve on anything more than a friendly basis, wouldn't he have told Matt not to say anything to Caitlin about Eve being at Montana Agricultural College? So, if it was so out in the open, she was fairly sure that nothing serious could be going on between them.

But Caitlin was still upset that Jed had lied to her. And in a very definite way, he had. He had lied by omission. He'd had plenty of chances to tell her about Eve, and he hadn't. So, it was as if he were trying to keep Eve's presence a secret. And hadn't she and Jed made a pact to always be completely honest with each other? Suddenly she felt the ache begin at the back of her throat again. They had even talked about honesty again before he'd flown back to Montana. Had he known, even then, that Eve would be going to the same school with him?

She had to know—and right away. Sitting up, she threw back the covers and jumped to her feet. Reaching for her robe, she glanced at the clock on her bedside table. Twenty minutes to ten. That meant it was twenty minutes to eight where he was. Maybe that was too early to call?

No—Jed was an early riser. Even though it was Saturday, he'd probably be up. She crossed to her desk, picked up the phone and went into the closet with it. She sat down inside and pulled the door almost shut so her conversation wouldn't bother Louise.

She dialed the long-distance number and waited while it rang ten, then twelve times.

"Hello. Hello," she said softly. "May I please speak to Jed Michaels?"

There was a muffled grunt on the other end of the line, then the sound of the receiver banging down on something hard. A faraway male voice called, "Jed! Hey, Jed, wake up." She heard someone knocking on a door. "Phone call."

Caitlin waited. She closed her eyes and leaned back against the wall, mentally telling herself to keep her breathing slow and even. But in the silence, with the receiver cupped tightly to her ear, she could hear the racing of her heart.

"Yeah—hello, who's this?" Jed's sleepy voice came over the line.

"Hi, Jed!" She tried to make herself sound cheerful. "It's me, Caitlin."

"Oh, Caitlin. Hi! It's you. Why are you whispering?"

"I don't want to disturb my roommate. Did I wake you up?"

"Well, actually, yes. You did."

"Out late last night?" She was keeping it light.

"Yeah. A bunch of us went out. You know, just fooling around. Then, when we came back here, we ended up talking until about four."

"Oh? Anyone I know?"

"Let me think. Oh, right. I think you met a couple of the guys this summer—Chuck Williams and Andy Hodes."

"A night out with the guys, huh?"

"Yes!" There was a pause. "Caitlin, did you call me up to ask who I went out with last night?"

As a matter of fact, yes. "Oh, of course not," she said quickly. "I was simply making conversation." She twisted her finger through the curly phone cord. There was an edge to her voice. "I just wanted to say hi, that's all. Is that some kind of crime?"

"Hey, I'm sorry. Forgive me, okay? I guess I'm being kind of grumpy. I'm still half-asleep."

"You want me to hang up?"

"No—no, of course not! Just don't jump on me with a whole bunch of questions—like you're grilling me or something."

"Jed, I wasn't doing that!"

"Well, it sounded like it."

Is he being overly defensive? she asked herself. "Hey, look, I'm sorry. I didn't mean to sound that way." She paused, twisting the cord again. "It's just that—well—I haven't gotten a letter from you in almost two weeks. I started to get worried, that's all."

"Hey, now it's my turn to apologize." His voice was contrite. "I've been up to my eyeballs in work on a project. I've been working night and day on it for the past two weeks. I just didn't have time to sit down and really concentrate on writing you. But that's over now. One of the reasons I went out last night was to celebrate— it's finished."

"I'm glad to hear that. Was it your own project, or were you working with someone?"

There was a long silence on the other end. Finally Jed asked, "Have you been talking to Matt?"

"What has that got to do with anything?"

"Matt told you about Eve, didn't he?"

"Yes." She gripped the phone. "Is there any reason why he shouldn't have?"

"Yes—no—uh, yes! Because I knew you'd get angry, I suppose."

"The only reason I'm angry is that you didn't tell me Eve was there at school with you. By the way"—her voice turned decidedly cool—"just what is Eve doing there, anyway?"

"She's going to school, Caitlin," Jed replied evenly. "The same as I'm going to school and you're going to school. She's working toward a degree."

And something besides a degree, Jed. "I suppose

105

Montana Agricultural College is the only school in the state?"

"Be realistic, Caitlin. It's a great school. And Eve wants to be a rancher. What do you want her to do, go to Colorado just so she won't be near me?"

Yes. Yes. Yes! "No, but do you have to work together on the same project?"

"It was assigned." Jed sighed heavily. "Caitlin," he said, "listen to me for a minute. I know how Eve behaved this summer, but she's changed. She honestly has. She told me how much she regrets what happened between you two, and she says she wishes you were here so she could apologize to you in person. Furthermore, I'm really glad I got to work with her on the project. I couldn't have asked for a better partner."

Caitlin was completely and totally speechless. Pulling the receiver away from her ear, she looked at it as though she couldn't believe what she had heard. How could Jed be so gullible? If even one tiny, nasty little hair on Eve's head had changed, then Jed had witnessed a true miracle. And Caitlin was very, very skeptical of miracles.

"Caitlin?"

"I'm here, Jed."

"Well?"

Caitlin looked out the closet door. Louise was stirring. "Well, I think I'd better get off the phone, Jed. I'm disturbing Louise, and I don't want to be selfish."

"Oh, sure—sure, I understand." Jed hesitated, as though he couldn't decide whether or not she was angry with him. "Uh, Caitlin?"

"I'd better go, Jed." She forced a light, easy note into her voice. "I'm sorry, again, that I woke you. Why don't you go back to bed and get some more sleep." She hung up on him just as she heard him start to say something else.

The second she put the receiver down, she wanted to snatch it up again. But she told herself that she had hung up on him for a reason. She wanted him to wonder what had gone wrong and to worry about it. She wanted him to be so concerned that he would sit down and write her a letter before he did anything else.

As she carried the phone over to her desk, her mood changed from frustration to anger. And she took her anger out on the phone, slamming it down on her desk before she remembered Louise was still asleep in the other bed.

"Yipes!" Louise jumped halfway out of bed, then fell back so that she was sitting on the edge. "Good grief! What is going on? Is there a fire? A panty raid? Isn't this Saturday?" She blinked, trying to focus her sleep-filled eyes.

"Oh, Louise, I'm sorry." Caitlin was contrite. "It was me. I slammed the phone down on the desk."

"How come?" Louise stared at her, pushing her tumbled cornsilk hair away from her face. "What happened?"

"It's Jed!" Caitlin took a deep breath. "I just called him." She threw her hands up in the air. "Ohhh, I'm so furious!"

"Excuse me, but the last I heard, you were madly in love with him! Okay, wait. I get it now." She nodded. "He's done something you don't like. Give me a second to pull myself together. I'm still half-asleep. Oh, now I remember. He hasn't written in a couple of weeks. And you called to find out why, right?"

"Right!" Caitlin began to pace. "And you know why he hasn't written?" She stopped pacing and planted her fists on her hips. "I'll tell you why. Because he's been so wrapped up with his old girlfriend—remember that horrible girl I told you about, the one who cut my saddle so that I'd lose the race?"

"Yeah, yeah!" Louise nodded. "I remember. So, go on. What's she doing with Jed?" So, Louise thought, as things started to become clear to her, Caitlin had somehow found out about Eve and Jed. But from whom? she wondered. Jed? Or Matt? And just how much did she actually know? Well, Louise thought, she had better listen and find out, before she started spilling Julian's version.

"Actually, I found out yesterday afternoon

that she's going to the same school as Jed. And that really got me upset because—because I felt as if he'd lied to me. Jed never said a word about Eve. But I didn't want to tell you about it, since there was the party—"

"And you didn't want to ruin anyone's time by acting depressed. Oh, Caitlin, how sweet and thoughtful of you." She gave Caitlin a sympathetic look. "So that's why your eyes were all red yesterday afternoon. You were crying, weren't you?"

"Um-hmm," Caitlin admitted. "But now I'm over that. Now I'm just totally furious. When we were on the phone just now, he was actually defending her. He was telling me what a great person she has become!" Angrily, she shook her head, so that her dark hair whipped across her face. "I don't believe it! I just don't believe it!"

Louise couldn't help smiling. To cover it up, she dropped her head forward so that her face was hidden. With an effort, she forced the smile off her face and looked up again. "That's terrible! Oh, Caitlin, how awful for you."

"Oh, Louise, it really *is* awful." Caitlin had stopped shaking her head and was standing there, looking dejected. It was as if all the anger had suddenly drained away, leaving her unsure of what to do. "I feel so helpless. He's two thousand miles away. And she's there with him, and she used to be his girlfriend, and I know she'll do anything to get him back. I just know it."

Louise thought she saw tears beginning to well up in Caitlin's eyes. *Now,* she thought, *now is the time to strike, to twist the knife.* "Caitlin"—she made her voice sound understanding—"you know, maybe it's really for the best that you found out this way, straight from Jed, before you found it out from"—she hesitated, then put emphasis on the next words—"anyone else."

"What do you mean, Louise? Are you trying to say that there really is something going on between Jed and Eve? Louise, do you know something you're not telling me? Because if you do, I'd certainly appreciate hearing it. Right now."

"All right, I guess you should know." Louise patted the vacant spot on the bed beside her. "Come on, sit down and I'll tell you."

Not taking her eyes off Louise's face, Caitlin walked across the room slowly. She sat down. "But how could you find out something about Jed and Eve? Something I don't even know about?"

"I heard it from Julian last night."

"Julian?"

"Yes, Julian," Louise said, gently taking Caitlin's hand. "I wish I didn't have to be the one to tell you this, but I guess you'd have found out eventually. You see, Julian knows a friend of

Jed's here at school. And Jed wrote his friend that he's seeing a lot of Eve." She felt Caitlin shudder. "I'm terribly sorry, Caitlin. But I did try to warn you about long-distance relationships." She let go of Caitlin's hand and put her arm around her shoulders. "So what are you going to do?"

Caitlin shook her head slowly. "I don't know, Louise. I just can't seem to think straight right now." She turned to look Louise in the eye. "But thank you for telling me the truth. I can guess where Julian got his information. And right now, I don't exactly think of this person as a friend."

Of course she means Matt Jenks, Louise gloated silently. Oh, everything was working out so well. Now Caitlin wouldn't be speaking to Matt. And she would never find out that she and Julian were making the whole thing up. Louise pulled her arm away from Caitlin's shoulders, no longer feeling right about leaving it there. She felt a stab of guilt go through her.

Pulling one knee up to her chin, she shifted sideways and put some space between the two of them. "You're right, Caitlin. You can't think about Jed right now. What you need is some distance from the problem. Give things time to cool." She smiled. "And I think I've got the perfect idea. Since the weather has cleared Julian and I can do what we planned and drive to

Leesburg today, to go to a concert. Afterward, we're planning to stop at this really great place for spaghetti—you know how I adore spaghetti. It's just going to be one of those relaxing kind of days, and I think you should come with us. How does that sound?"

"Oh, thank you, Louise." Caitlin smiled weakly. "That's really sweet of you to invite me. But I don't want to intrude. I mean, you and Julian don't want me along on your date."

"Don't be silly." Louise drew both knees up to her chin and wrapped her arms around them. "Of course I want you to come. I wouldn't have suggested it if I didn't. And I'm positive Julian will feel the same way. After all, he did want you to have dinner with us last night. And since that fell through, just consider this as a rain check. As for its being a date, it's not—not in the sense you mean, anyway. We're just friends—like you and Hal."

"Oh, but I thought—I mean, the way you first described him to me—that he was so tall, dark, and—"

"Handsome," Louise finished for her. "I know. And he is. I admit that, at first, I thought our relationship was going to turn into the romance of the century. But then Julian made it perfectly clear that, for him, medicine comes first. He doesn't have time for romance—at least not right now. And I honestly don't mind. He's so interesting just to be with." She gave a light shrug. "As for romance, there are plenty of other guys on campus."

"Oh! Well, then—" Caitlin hesitated, frowning as she thought.

She's weakening, Louise thought to herself, delighted. And that meant she would be able to deliver Caitlin right into Julian's hands, just as he'd asked. "So?" she asked eagerly. "Then you'll go with us?"

"Yes." Caitlin nodded. "I'll go. If Jed can fool around with other girls, then maybe I should start having a little fun myself."

11

Caitlin decided on the strategy she was going to use on Jed while she was having dinner with Julian and Louise.

As they drove to the concert in Louise's white Mazda, Caitlin was silent, feeling very much the outsider. But by the time the group took their first break, Caitlin's spirits had lifted considerably. The music had left her feeling buoyant and full of energy—ready to have fun.

And her mood was still light when they stopped at a cozy little restaurant called Roberto's. It was on the verge of being scruffy, with worn red-and-white-checked tablecloths and candles stuck into Chianti bottles on each table. Dusty clusters of plastic grapes hung from plastic vines that were twined around the exposed wooden beams of the ceiling.

Julian did the ordering. It was obvious, when the food arrived, why Roberto's was such a popular place. To start, they had a green salad with deeply veined blue cheese and a tangy house dressing. Then came the homemade pasta with a thick, rich meat sauce. And to go with it, they were given crisp bread sticks, warm from the oven. Julian ordered a bottle of red Italian table wine for the three of them. Although Louise and Caitlin rarely drank, they decided that the meal wouldn't seem authentic without a little wine.

There was a jukebox in one corner with space for dancing in front of it. Julian danced first with Louise, then with Caitlin.

Finding herself in his arms, Caitlin realized it was the first time they had actually touched. The hand that took hers was warm and strong, with long, tapering fingers—the hand of an artist or a surgeon, she thought.

As their bodies fit together to move with the slow rhythm of the song that was playing, Caitlin felt an odd sensation. It was as if she had known Julian for years. But that was impossible. Perhaps it was just that the name Stokes was so familiar since she had worked with little Kathy Stokes over the summer in Rock Ridge, Caitlin reasoned. Still. . . . She thought for a moment and then decided to say something.

"Do you have any relatives in West Virginia?" she asked. Her voice was muffled against his chest, which she'd leaned her cheek against.

Julian's eyes grew wide, and a wave of panic

swept through him. But his voice when he replied was calm. "No, not that I know of. Why?"

Caitlin pulled away from Julian and looked up into his gray eyes. "I guess this sounds silly, but you seem awfully familiar—as if we've met before. And there was this family named Stokes in the town in West Virginia where I worked last summer. I just thought that maybe— It does sound a little crazy, doesn't it?"

"Not at all. I'm always amazed by what a small world it is and how many people know people in common, especially at Carleton Hill. But as far as I know, I don't have any relatives outside the D.C. area. I know there are other Stokeses around, though. It's not that uncommon a name."

"I guess not. It doesn't matter anyway," Caitlin replied.

The beat of the music changed, and Julian pulled her closer as they whirled around the small dance floor. For just a few seconds, Caitlin could feel his heart beating through the double layer of sweaters that separated them. "You dance well," he said, his voice sounding almost formal as he relaxed his hold on her.

"Thank you." Caitlin felt confused. He had thrown her off guard. One moment he was holding her in a tight embrace and the next he was complimenting her in the exact way her dancing master used to when she was twelve.

After Julian returned her to the table, he led Louise out onto the floor. Caitlin sat sipping her wine as she watched them together. She noticed that Julian didn't seem to be holding Louise as closely as he had held her. But, then, too, the song was faster. That had to be the reason.

It was strange, she thought, how she hadn't really recognized Julian when he had come for them earlier that day. She knew that she had talked to him the day before. But she couldn't recall from that meeting exactly how he looked. And that really was strange, because Julian Stokes was so striking and so different from the other boys on campus. It wasn't just that he was good-looking; he was handsome in such a sophisticated, mature way that she couldn't stop staring at him. His slate-colored eyes seemed to have the power to look inside her and see what she was thinking. It was unnerving, yet thrilling to Caitlin at the same time.

Then, as she sat alone, watching Louise and Julian, she thought about how angry she felt when Jed had finally told her about Eve's being at school with him. And then she realized that anger had only been masking her real emotion— jealousy. What if she used jealousy to get Jed back?

Handsome, sophisticated Julian would be the

perfect choice to make any boy insanely jealous. It was too bad he wasn't interested in dating. *No,* she told herself, *I could never use another person that way.* And, when she thought about it, she couldn't imagine Julian ever letting himself be used.

All she really had to do was write to Jed and tell him not to expect too many letters in the next few weeks because she was going to be too busy. Now that she was a pledge, she'd explain, she was just going to be involved in too many activities. In fact, in addition to her duties as a new member of both the art club and the French club, there was also a casual party the next night, at the Sigma house. And all the Kappa Kappa Deltas had been invited. Then Homecoming was in two weeks, which meant a parade and the first football game. And that night, there would be the big dance. She also remembered that Carol, her new sorority sister, had told her that Darrell Hart wanted to ask her to go to the dance with him. As a pledge, she was expected to attend. Why not go with one of the stars of the football team? she asked herself.

Caitlin listed all of her activities for the next two weeks in a letter she wrote to Jed that very night.

His response arrived on the Friday before Homecoming. She found the letter in her mailbox when she got back to the dorm after an afternoon of blowing up blue and white balloons and attaching them to the KKD float.

When she saw the return address on the corner of the envelope, a tiny thrill of excitement went through her. That he had answered so quickly could only mean one thing: her plan had worked; she had made him jealous. As she ran to the nearest couch, sat down, and ripped open the letter, she was already imagining what Jed had written: how much he loved her; how wrong he'd been about Eve; how Eve really was a terrible person; how he would never so much as look at her again. . . . But then she read what Jed had really written, and her stomach began to knot. The letter was not at all what she had expected. It was horrible and cold.

Caitlin—

I'll make this letter short. Since you said you'll be too busy to write much in the next few weeks, I take it that means you won't have the time to read my letters either.

I don't really know what's going on, Caitlin. I can only make guesses. But whatever it is, I don't like it.

First you call me at my dorm—so early in the morning that everyone wanted to know what the emergency was—just to check up on me. Then you follow that up with a letter telling me how busy you're going to be because of this sorority you've joined. Was the letter meant to make me jealous? If it was, I really don't appreciate it. I thought our relationship went much deeper.

Or perhaps what you're trying to say is that you've gone back to being the party girl you were when I first met you. If that's it, then you're obviously in the right place. Carleton Hill sounds like a real party school.

As for being too busy to write, I guess I'll be busy myself for a while. There's a rodeo coming up, and Eve and I are teaming up for the bulldogging and steer-roping events.

Well, do write if you ever have the time. And I'll try to do the same.

Jed

Slowly Caitlin reread the letter. Yes, she had read it right. Now he hated her. She had lost him. It was her own stupid fault. Oh, how she hated herself. Why had she ever thought she could make Jed jealous? He was much too smart. He had seen right through her. She regretted what she had done enormously. But now it was too late.

Letting the letter fall to her lap, she absently looked at her watch, noting the time. She should be upstairs right then, taking a shower and changing. She was due back at the KKD house for dinner in less than an hour. But the last thing she felt like doing was going there. All she really wanted to do was to go someplace where she could be alone—to think about Jed and the terrible mess she'd made of their relationship.

* * *

Somehow Caitlin managed to get through the festivities of Homecoming Weekend. When she thought about it later, it was only because she had been kept so busy that she barely had time to take a breath, let alone think.

There was a mad dash on the Saturday morning of Homecoming to put the finishing touches on the Kappa Kappa Delta float and get it to the start of the parade.

After the parade, there was a luncheon at the sorority house for the returning KKD alumnae. Then there was the game, which was exhausting because Caitlin found herself yelling and screaming each time Darrell carried the ball down to the end zone. And finally that evening there was the dance. Caitlin wore an emerald green taffeta dress from Paris that swished softly as she danced. Although everyone told her she looked beautiful and her smile was bright, she felt cheated. She should have been enjoying herself. Homecoming was one of the biggest social events of the whole year. But all she could think of as she danced in Darrell's arms was Jed.

The week that followed was more of the same. Caitlin's schedule was tight. What she had told Jed in her letter hadn't been far from the truth.

As a pledge, she was expected to spend a certain number of hours at the KKD house in a study group. The sessions were held because the pledges were expected to maintain high grades. That wasn't difficult for Caitlin; she had graduated at the top of her class in high school. But still, the structured hours took a lot of her time. Then there was dinner at the house three times a week, and meetings, and running errands for the actives—plus all of her classes.

On Friday morning, miraculously, she had two hours between classes that were all hers. Feeling almost selfish, but knowing she needed the time to herself, she went to the student union, bought a cup of hot tea, and carried it to a small table in a far corner. She piled her books in a huge stack on the Formica surface, hoping they would discourage anyone from joining her. Then she propped open a textbook and pretended to study. Behind the book she was allowing her thoughts to drift at random.

Moments later, Julian came into the union to grab a quick cup of coffee before he headed off to a four-hour chemistry lab. He spotted Caitlin immediately. As he stood in line to pay for his coffee, he watched her. At first he thought he wouldn't approach her. She seemed to be engrossed in her studying, her head down, the dark curtain of her hair hiding her face. But when she raised her head and rested her chin on one cupped hand, he could not help but see the sad look on her exquisite face. He changed his mind and walked over to her.

"Hello," he said, coming to stand beside her table.

"Oh—hello!" Caitlin glanced up, startled for a moment. The look in her luminous blue eyes reminded him of a startled forest creature.

Julian smiled. "You looked so lonely. I thought I'd join you while I drink my coffee." He slid the piled-up books to one side, taking it for granted that she wouldn't refuse him. "You don't mind, do you?"

"Well—" Caitlin hesitated.

But he had already sat down. "Art history?" He gestured toward the book she still had propped up in front of her. "Do you like it?"

"Yes, I do." She nodded vaguely, thinking that she should just tell him to go away. But then she shut the book and pushed it to one side. Now there was a cleared space between them. "It's one of my favorite courses."

"I've always wanted to take it," Julian said. "I've just never gotten around to it."

"I suppose you wouldn't. I imagine a premed major has to take too many science classes."

"That's true." Julian took a sip of his coffee, then put down the cup and reached his hand across the table to rest his fingers close to hers. "Caitlin, the real reason I came over here was because you looked so unhappy, so sad. I was certain something had to be troubling you. If there is, I'd like to do whatever I can to help. You know, sometimes just talking helps."

"Thank you, Julian. That's very kind. But there's really nothing wrong." Caitlin looked down at Julian's fingers. They were close to hers—not touching, yet there seemed to be a kind of energy flowing from his fingertips into hers as they rested on the tabletop. She felt as if someone were gently massaging the back of her neck. Raising her eyes, she looked into his. They were so kind. She was sure he could see inside her mind and read her innermost thoughts. She found herself wanting to tell him about Jed. . . .

Julian's coffee was cold by the time Caitlin had finished, but his hand was still resting in the same place. Now he lifted it and placed it over hers. "Caitlin, listen to me. I don't think it's over between you and Jed. He sounds like someone who's worth the extra effort it will take for you to write to him and level with him. I'm sure he still loves you. Love doesn't get destroyed because of a little distance or a small misunderstanding. You simply need to find a way back to each other."

"Oh, Julian!" Caitlin's eyes glistened with hope. "Do you really think so?"

"Of course I do." Julian gently squeezed her hand.

"Then that's exactly what I'll do." Caitlin felt happy for the first time in days. "I have some time right now. I'll write him a letter and mail it before I go to my next class."

12

On Saturday, the hazing that the pledges had all been wondering about was sprung on them. Three KKD members went around and woke up the pledges—including, of course, Louise and Caitlin. And, without letting any of them so much as wash their faces or brush their hair, they herded the girls over to the Omega Psi house, where they were ordered to cook breakfast for the whole fraternity.

"Wow! Now that I know what you look like when you get up in the morning, I think I'd like to pin you," Darrell told Caitlin. She had just finished setting down a plate of bacon, eggs, and biscuits in front of him.

"How terribly sweet of you, Darrell," Caitlin replied. She winked at Louise, who was standing on the other side of the table, serving Jeffrey Burns his third helping of sausage and biscuits. "Is that a real, honest-to-goodness proposal? Are you actually asking me to be engaged to be engaged to you? I can't begin to tell you how excited that makes me feel. My heart is just going thump, thump, thump."

Caitlin was feeling absolutely great, fully ready to exchange quips with Darrell or any of the other guys in the fraternity. Ever since mailing that letter to Jed the day before, she had decided that life was definitely worth living again. After Julian had talked to her, she realized she'd been making a mistake by letting her relationship with Jed disintegrate, instead of acting positively to improve it. Although the letter she wrote had not been an out-and-out apology, she was fairly certain he would get her message.

"I think you'd better forget about Caitlin," Louise was warning Darrell. "Concentrate on someone else. She's in the midst of making up with her boyfriend."

"You mean that cowboy out West?" Darrell glanced up at Caitlin for confirmation. She nodded. "Well"—he leaned an elbow on the table—"I wonder how long that would last if he found out that at this very moment you are serving breakfast to the star of the Carleton Hill Militia football team, dressed only in a pair of the prettiest silk pajamas I've ever seen."

"I'm sure he'd understand," Caitlin replied with an easy smile.

"Hey! How many pairs of silk pajamas have

you seen, Darrell?" someone yelled from another table.

"And hey! Who says *you're* the star of the Militia?" a boy across the table objected. "You never would have made that winning touchdown if I hadn't tackled that fullback who was about to head you off."

"Yeah, and don't forget who passed you the ball!"

"And, like, don't forget our excellent defense!"

All at once Darrell found himself being pelted with biscuits and pieces of toast. Caitlin yelped and ducked out of the line of fire. Reaching over, she grabbed Louise's hand. "Come on, Louise," she called, laughing, "I think breakfast is over."

"She's happy again," Louise said in a dry tone. She was talking to Julian in one of the smaller TV lounges in the union. The TV set was off, and they were the only ones in the room. "You should have seen her at the hazing Saturday. She could have wrapped the entire fraternity around her little finger if she'd wanted to."

"It's all right, Louise," Julian soothed her. "Don't worry. It won't last. She's only feeling that way because she thinks everything is going to be fine between her and Jed. I convinced her

128

that a letter would do the trick, but I was just setting her up."

"But what if the letter does what you told her it would, and they do get back together?" Louise frowned. "And, anyway, I'm not so sure we're doing the right thing. I mean, as long as she's going with Jed, she's not dating any other guys. So—"

"You're losing sight of what we originally started out to do," Julian chided. "We're trying to flatten Caitlin's ego. We want to make her feel hopelessly insecure. Think, Louise. Just a minute ago you said she was the center of attention at the Sigma house. Now, why do you think that was?"

"Because she was feeling so great about Jed?" Louise asked in a small voice. She knew the answer already.

"That's right." Reaching over, Julian squeezed her hand reassuringly.

The way he touched her hand, Louise felt almost as if she were an obedient dog being patted for having learned a new trick. It irritated her. "All right, Julian," she snapped. "Just tell me what it is you want me to do."

"It's very simple, Louise. All you have to do is let me know when Jed's letter arrives." Louise watched his mouth as the corners turned up in a persuasive smile. Funny, she thought, how that smile no longer warmed her the way it used to.

"That, and let me know what he's written. I want you to read the letter."

Jed's letter to Caitlin arrived a week after Julian and Louise's conversation. Caitlin tore it open with trembling hands. She read it through once, quickly. Then she read it again more slowly, searching for any small clue to his feelings that she might have missed the first time. But there was none. She glanced down the page again, skipping a detailed description of the rodeo. *At least he didn't mention Eve*, Caitlin thought hopefully.

Nothing really changes around here. I'm working hard. Some of my classes are interesting, some aren't. I call my dad often. He complains that the cold weather's bothering him more than usual this year, but other than that he insists that he's feeling fine. It's difficult to know if he's telling the truth, or not. I guess all I can do is to keep in touch, and go home whenever possible. But I worry, of course.

I hope everything is going well for you, Caitlin. And thanks for your letter. Write again when you have time.

Jed

The letter puzzled Caitlin. On one hand, it was a good sign that he'd written back at all. On the other hand, his distant tone was not a good sign. After going back and forth about it for a while, she decided that the best thing she could do would be to wait and see what happened next. And write more letters.

"It came," Louise reported. She spoke into the phone in a low tone even though she was using the pay phone in an empty corner of the dorm lobby. She had decided not to use the phone in her room.

"So?" Julian said tersely.

"So, I read it." She shrugged, although she knew he couldn't see her over the phone. "Well, I really don't see why Caitlin thinks this guy is so terrific. I mean, except for the fact that he's gorgeous, he is really dull. At least his letter is."

"What do you mean? Come on, Louise, be more specific."

"Well, it wasn't very long. Only one page. And it was all about horses and a rodeo. He didn't even sign it 'love.' Just 'Jed.'"

"Did he mention anything about Eve?"

"Huh-uh." Louise shook her head. "Just as I said, bor-ing."

"Good!"

"Good?"

"Yes. Thank you, Louise. I'll talk to you later."

"But Jul—" Louise began, confused, her brow furrowed. But Julian had already hung up.

* * *

Julian found Caitlin as she was coming out of the library. He paused just out of her sight to watch her descend the stairs, and he was struck anew by the freshness of her beauty. The afternoon was blustery, with lowering gray clouds. In a bright red pea jacket, white fisherman's sweater, and slim-cut jeans, her blue backpack slung over one shoulder, she was the one radiant spot of color in an otherwise drab scene.

Measuring his steps so that he would meet her when she reached the bottom of the stairs, he found himself almost regretting what he was about to do. He thought of the time when he was a small boy and had set out to capture a beautiful red bird. He had built a trap, then quietly waited. He had only wanted to hold the bird in his hand, to feel its softness. And he had wondered how such a tiny thing could fly so strongly and so high. But the bird had struggled in the handmade trap. And, before Julian could set it free, it had broken a wing.

"Hello, Caitlin."

"Oh—Julian!" A bit startled at his sudden appearance, she nevertheless managed to smile up at him. Her cheeks were flushed with the early-November cold, and her blue eyes sparkled. "Are you going into the library?"

"No," Julian said, smiling. "Actually I was looking for you."

"Me?" Caitlin's look was curious as she asked, "Why?"

Instead of answering her question, he asked, "Are you free now? Do you have time for a cup of coffee?" He reached up and touched her cheek. "This wind's cold. You look as though you could use something hot to drink."

"Well"—Caitlin glanced at her watch and frowned as she calculated—"I suppose I do have a few minutes. My next class isn't for about half an hour." She looked back up at Julian's face. "You still haven't told me what you want to talk to me about."

"Why don't we go over to the Hearthside?" Taking her backpack from her, he slung it over his shoulder, then lightly grasped her arm and began to walk with her. "I'd rather wait to explain it, if you don't mind."

Ten minutes later they were at a table at the Hearthside. Nearby, a fire burned cheerfully in the fireplace, behind a polished brass and glass screen. A waitress had just brought them two mugs of hot coffee.

Glancing through the window at the people walking by, their coat collars pulled up, hands plunged deep into their pockets, Julian commented, "There's a real chill in the air."

"Julian!" Caitlin leaned forward. "What is it

133

you want to tell me?" Julian tilted his head back as he looked directly at her. "I can tell from your eyes that it's serious," she said. "Tell me, please!"

"All right." Julian took a deep breath, then let out a long sigh. He lowered his eyelids as if trying to shield his painful thoughts from her. "I really hate hurting you like this, Caitlin." He looked up, his expression full of concern. "But as your friend, I think you have a right to know what's going on."

"What's going on?"

"It's Jed."

"Jed!" Caitlin drew her breath in sharply. "What about Jed?"

Julian traced a small circle with his coffee cup. "You know that I'm in a study group with Matt Jenks, don't you?"

"Yes, sure," Caitlin said.

"Well, he told me something about Jed that you should know. I'm sworn to secrecy on this, but I like you so much, Caitlin. I—I just can't stand to see someone hurt you like this." He paused long enough to shake his head slowly in a gesture of regret. "It seems that Jed and Eve recently went away together to go skiing. They spent a weekend at a lodge in the Rockies. Apparently, according to Jed's letter to Matt, it was a very cozy time." Julian glanced toward the cheerful blaze in the fireplace, then back at

134

Caitlin. "I know, hearing this hurts. But I figured it would hurt even more if I let Jed go on playing you for a fool."

"No! No." Caitlin shook her head dumbly. "I just can't believe it."

"Well, if you want to, you can ask Matt, of course." He reached across the table to take her hand, holding it warmly in his. "Though then he'll know that I broke my word about keeping this a secret from you." Julian felt fairly safe in speaking as he did. He was certain Caitlin would never do such a thing. And, even if she did, what he had told her was true—at least the part about Eve and Jed going skiing together. He just hadn't mentioned that there had been a group of about sixty other students with them. "But, believe me, I would understand if you talked to Matt," he added, giving her hand a tender squeeze.

"Oh, it's not that I don't believe you. Of course I do." Caitlin's voice was thick with pain. "It's— it's that I don't want to believe that Jed—" She stopped, unable to say more.

"I know. I know you'd never tell Matt," Julian said. "Caitlin, I'm so sorry." He watched as she turned her head away from him and stared into the fire. A tiny flicker of the firelight was reflected in the single tear that rolled down her cheek. Julian glanced away. He had succeeded in the first step of his plan.

13

 ⌣

"Ginny?" Caitlin twisted the phone cord in her fingers. "Hi! Is that you?"

"Caitlin? Hi!" Ginny's familiar voice came over the line. "How're you doing?"

"Okay, I guess." Caitlin found herself frowning at the semi-lie. "Listen—could, I mean—would you like to come visit this weekend? I really need an old friend right now."

"This weekend?" Ginny paused. "I'm so bad with dates. But isn't your eighteenth birthday around now? Don't you have to go to Ryan Acres for it?"

"You're right. My birthday is coming up—on Monday, as a matter of fact. But I'm not going home. I'm just not up to dealing with Colin Wollman right now. So when my grandmother called, I told her that I had a lot of really tough exams to study for."

"Well, what about a party? Is anyone throwing a party for your eighteenth?"

"Huh-uh. I don't want one, so I haven't told anyone here that it's my birthday. And if you come up, you have to promise you won't tell anyone, okay?"

"I promise. And I'd really love to come. In fact, I could stand being with an old friend for a few days myself." Caitlin heard Ginny sigh over the phone. "I've just got to get away from here for a while. I don't know what to do. I think I'm going to have to find a new place to board Cinnamon."

Caitlin heard a note of distress in her friend's voice. "Ginny! Why? What are you talking about? What happened?"

"I broke up with Win. He's such a creep. I can't believe I let myself be fooled for so long."

"What do you mean?"

"He hates horses!" Ginny's words exploded in Caitlin's ear. "Can you believe that? He only plays polo because he thinks it's important for social reasons. He's a social climber. And I fell for him. I could just kick myself."

"Oh, Ginny, I'm so sorry," Caitlin said softly. "Listen, just come up. We'll cry on each other's shoulders."

"Caitlin? Something's wrong with you, too, isn't it?" There was a second or two of silence on the line. "It's not Jed, is it?" More silence. "What happened?"

"Can you come?" Caitlin asked in a small voice.

"You bet," Ginny assured her.

"I'll tell you everything as soon as you get here."

Ginny arrived early Saturday morning, with a gift for Caitlin, a pale blue angora sweater with white trim.

"I love it!" Caitlin told Ginny, turning around and around with the sweater held up in front of her. Then she folded it up and put it in a drawer. "I'll wear it to dinner at my sorority house tomorrow night."

"I'm so glad you like it," Ginny said. "I'm never really sure what to get you. You have so many clothes, and you've got such great taste."

"*You've* got great taste!" Caitlin hugged her friend. "Besides, I'd love anything you got me—just because it came from you."

"Thanks." Ginny hugged her back. "So, did you say something about a tennis game? I packed my whites, and my racquet's down in the car."

"Great!" Caitlin nodded. "I've reserved an indoor court in about an hour. I thought we could work off our frustrations, then take a shower and go get some lunch."

"That sounds like a terrific idea," Ginny agreed. "I always cry better over something rich and gooey. But then, you know me whenever I'm miserable—the first thing I do is pig out on desserts. Considering everything I've stuffed into my mouth this past week, I should look like a blimp by now. It's a good thing I'm not the type who gains weight easily. I think my craving may lead me to a big slice of apple crumb cake today."

"You don't have apple crumb cake?" Ginny looked at the waitress disappointedly. "Hmm. Well, how about chocolate cream pie?" The waitress nodded. "Great. Then I'll have a piece of that. And make it a la mode, please."

Caitlin put her hand up to her mouth to stifle a laugh until the waitress left. Then she burst into giggles. "I don't believe you, Ginny. Who ever heard of chocolate cream pie a la mode? I take back everything that I said about your having good taste."

"You were talking about clothes." Ginny sniffed. Then she grinned. "I told you, I'm working out my disappointment about Win." A serious look came over her face. Leaning forward, she put her elbows on the table. "Okay, now that I've spilled out my tale of woe about Win, the Closet Horse Hater, it's your turn.

What else makes you so sure that Jed is really seeing Eve?"

Caitlin frowned, thinking, as she ran her finger around the rim of her coffee cup. "Well, actually, there's not much more to tell. I think you know just about everything now."

"Oh, Caitlin." Ginny sighed. "I know how awful you must feel. And I just can't believe that Jed would do something so terrible." She leaned back, a thoughtful expression on her face. "If I were you, I'd be absolutely sure he'd actually gone skiing with her. I mean, you got this information from someone else, after all. You weren't there, looking over Jed and Eve's shoulders."

"I know. That's what I was thinking, too," Caitlin agreed. "So that's why I called him."

"You called Jed and out and out accused him?" Ginny's eyes widend.

"Well, not exactly." Caitlin shook her head. "Nothing that obvious. I made it a casual call. And I sort of casually mentioned how I'd heard that Eve was a great skiier."

"Ahh! Very sneaky." Ginny smiled. "So, what happened?"

Caitlin gave a little sigh. "He said that what I'd heard was wrong—"

"But that's great!" Ginny interrupted.

"Hang on. Let me finish," Caitlin said. "The reason Jed gave for what I'd heard being wrong is that Eve's not a *good* skiier. She's just a beginner.''

"That rat!" Ginny narrowed her eyes. "That means he really did spend the weekend with Eve."

"I know. At least, I know that's what it sounds like. But now I'm really confused. Think about it, Ginny. If you were going out with someone who was two thousand miles away and you decided to spend a weekend fooling around with someone else, would you mention anything about the weekend to the person you were going out with?"

"God, you're right!" Ginny stared at her friend. "I never would have thought about it that way. So?"

"So, I'm not any better off than I was before I called him."

"Do you have any idea what you're going to do now?"

"I've already done about the only thing I can do," Caitlin said. "I wrote him a letter, a nice, chatty letter. Now I'm waiting for an answer to that. Remember, Ginny, my birthday's on Monday. He can't very well forget my birthday, can he?"

Ginny's eyes narrowed. "He wouldn't dare!"

Just then, the waitress returned to their table. "I'm sorry to have taken so long," she apologized, "but we seem to be out of chocolate cream pie. Is there any other kind you'd like a la mode?"

"Hmmm." Ginny thought for a second, then looked up brightly. "Well, how about banana cream?"

After lunch Caitlin and Ginny decided to go back to Caitlin's dorm. They were almost there when they ran into Louise and Julian.

Even before Caitlin stopped to greet them Ginny's gaze was already riveted on Julian. He seemed too handsome to be real. And, as Caitlin made the introductions, Ginny found herself responding automatically. Instead of paying attention to what she was saying, Ginny was staring into Julian's smoldering gray eyes. She had never met a more handsome guy in her whole life.

"Ginny's an old high-school friend of Caitlin's," Louise was saying. "They went to Highgate Academy together. Now she goes to UVA."

"Ah, the University of Virginia." Julian smiled and extended his hand to her. "That's one of the places I'm considering for medical school."

"Uh—oh, really?" Ginny swallowed nervously as she took Julian's hand. *How fabulous*, she thought. "The medical school has a great reputation."

"So I've heard."

"Uhh—" Ginny suddenly realized she had nothing more to say. She searched her brain for an intelligent remark to make.

Fortunately, Louise spoke up just then about something else. "Oh, by the way, Caitlin, there's someone waiting for you in the lobby."

"Who is it? Do you know?"

"Some guy in a chauffeur's uniform. He says his name is Rollins."

"Rollins is here?" Caitlin was suddenly terrified that something might be wrong with her grandmother. "Did he say why he's here?"

"He didn't have to." Louise grinned. "He's got a huge gift-wrapped box with him."

"Oh." Caitlin gave a sigh of relief, then smiled. "Well, I guess I'd better hurry up and find out what it is."

"I know I sure would." Louise waved as she and Julian started down the walk.

"Do you think it's a birthday present?" Ginny wondered as they walked away from Julian and Louise.

"Probably. But a big box? What could it be?"

"Yeah, I wonder," Ginny replied. But she wasn't thinking about what could be waiting for Caitlin. She was thinking about Julian—his heart-stopping smile, his thick dark hair, and especially his incredible gray eyes. She hoped she'd see him again soon—very soon.

As Caitlin and Ginny entered the dorm lobby,

it was easy to spot Rollins. He was sitting absolutely erect on the edge of one of the chairs in the center of the large, comfortable room. The box Louise had mentioned was on the floor beside him. It really was big. It was wrapped in silver foil and tied with red ribbon.

Seeing Caitlin and Ginny approach, the Ryans' chauffeur jumped to his feet and greeted them both respectfully. Then he bent down and picked up the box, placing it on the seat of the chair so Caitlin could open it easily.

"I was told to wait until you'd tried it on, Miss Ryan," Rollins said. "And, if it doesn't fit, I'm to return it to Ryan Acres so that it can be exchanged."

"Sounds interesting," Ginny commented, raising her eyebrows. "Hurry up and open it!"

The ribbon came right off when Caitlin pulled at it. She then lifted off the top and pushed the layers of tissue aside. "Oh, no!" she said in a disappointed tone as she saw the soft pile of luxurious fur that lay in front of her.

"Wow!" Ginny gasped. "It's a lynx coat."

"There must be some mistake," Caitlin said quietly. There was a small ivory-colored envelope lying on top of the coat, and she picked it up. She tore the flap up and pulled out the note that was inside. The writing was in her grandmother's flowing, distinctive script.

A little something for your special day.
Happy Birthday.

Love,
Grandmother

"I just don't understand," Caitlin said, shaking her head.

"What's not to understand?" Ginny asked. "It's a fantastic fur coat!"

"It's a lot of poor little dead animals," Caitlin countered. "Ginny, do you remember how I told you that when I was in Montana I accidentally killed a helpless little animal?" Ginny nodded. "When I looked into that poor creature's eyes as it was dying, I knew I could never, never wear fur again."

Ginny said softly, "Now I do remember your telling me that."

"And my grandmother knows because as soon as I went back home to Ryan Acres, I told her I wanted to give away all my furs."

"Then I don't understand." Ginny shook her head. "Who picked out the coat?"

"Colin!" Caitlin's eyes narrowed as she envisioned Colin Wollman selecting what he thought would be a suitable coat for Caitlin. She could imagine how he had told her grandmother he could take care of that little errand for her.

"Rollins"—she turned to the chauffeur—"I'd like you to take this coat back with you. But—I don't want you to deliver it to my grandmother."

Caitlin reached into her purse and took out a pen. Then, turning the note over, she quickly scribbled something onto the back of it. She put the note back into the box on top of the fur. "I want you to make sure that Mr. Wollman gets it. And be sure to tell him there's a message inside for my grandmother."

As soon as Rollins left, Ginny turned to Caitlin. "Okay, I can see you're up to something," she said, grinning. "What is it? Tell me what you wrote on the card, and just why you wanted to make sure that Colin was going to read it instead of your grandmother. That is what you're thinking he'll do, isn't it?"

"You're right. I wrote thanks to my grandmother. But then I said it was obvious that the store had made a mistake by sending what it did." Caitlin's mouth turned up in a wicked little smile. "Now let's see if Colin is capable of figuring out my real message."

"Ah-hah. You mean that he's not as smart as he thinks he is, huh?"

Caitlin smiled. "Exactly."

14

On Monday, Caitlin's birthday, she received a wonderful surprise. It was from her father.

A beautiful spray of white orchids in an antique Chinese vase was delivered, along with a small velvet jeweler's box. Inside the box was a gold pin in the shape of a wreath. The fine gold bands had been intertwined to form the leaves and twigs.

It was a lovely gift, and Caitlin knew that a lot of thought had gone into choosing the pin, as well as the vase and flowers.

On Tuesday Caitlin returned to the dorm to find something more had been delivered, a small package wrapped in plain brown paper. She knew instantly that it was from Colin. As she carried the box to her room, she wondered if he had understood the unwritten message she had sent him. She hoped so. She hoped he had received it loud and clear. If he had, then perhaps he wouldn't be so quick to act on her grandmother's behalf from then on.

Sitting down on the edge of her bed, she ripped off the paper. The name of the exclusive department store was the same as on the first box. She opened it. This time what greeted her was the glimmer of shiny silver. It was a wide, heavy, obviously expensive silver bracelet. It was almost impersonal in its lack of character. She picked it up and slipped in onto her wrist. It wasn't even her style. It was more suitable for an older, bigger-boned woman.

Underneath the bracelet was a folded piece of business stationery. Caitlin picked it up and unfolded the brief, typewritten note.

Dear Caitlin,
I do apologize for the error on the store's part. I hope the enclosed is more to your liking. If not, then please contact me at the office and I'll handle the exchange. I'm sure you'll agree that it would serve no purpose to bother your grandmother with the details of any further exchanges. I hope you had a happy birthday.
Colin Wollman

Putting down the note, she slipped the bracelet off her wrist and turned it around in her hands. As she did, she wondered how much trouble Colin had had to go to to discover the reason she had sent back the lynx coat. A lot, she hoped. And wasn't it just like him to latch onto

her excuse that the store had probably made a
mistake. As if a store of that prominence would
make such an enormous error.

She was about to drop the bracelet back into
the box when Louise came into the room.

"Oh, Caitlin!" Louise gasped, her eyes glitter-
ing with envy. "What a fabulous bracelet!"
Coming over to the bed, she reached for it and
held it up so that the light danced on the surface.
"Wow! I love it." She slipped it onto her arm.
"Mind if I try it on?" she asked, not waiting for
Caitlin's reply. "This is gorgeous." She held her
arm out, admiring the way it looked on her.
"Well, I'll tell you one thing. If I got something
like this for my birthday, I wouldn't ask for a
single other thing."

Caitlin gave her a vague smile. She was
thinking that she would give a dozen silver
bracelets in exchange for one inexpensive, corny
birthday card from Jed. Apparently he had
forgotten her eighteenth birthday. Unless, of
course something from him came in the afternoon mail. In another hour she could go downstairs and check.

When she did check, she found only one letter
in her box. It was from her grandmother, expres-
sing her pleasure that Caitlin had appreciated
her present.

Colin told me, when we breakfasted together
on Sunday, that you were delighted with the

gift. I must admit I did leave the choice up to him. He said he would check with his sister to see what she might suggest. As you know, Nicole owns that little boutique in Alexandria that caters to the college set.

Ah-hah! Caitlin thought with angry satisfaction. She had been right. Colin had been involved, and so had Nicole. It was obvious her grandmother hadn't seen the note she had sent. Her grandmother probably didn't even know what Colin had sent her as a present. After quickly scanning the rest of the letter, she stuffed it back into the envelope and put it on her desk. Leave it to Nicole to pick out a coat made of cat fur. It seemed so fitting because that was just the way she thought of Nicole—as a sneaky, slinky cat. Well, one of these days, either Colin or Nicole—or both of them—would make a slip. And then she herself would be there ready to pounce—to make sure her grandmother and father learned what Colin and Nicole were really like.

Each afternoon Caitlin checked the mail—her heart starting to race the minute she pushed through the lobby doors. But each day, when she approached the bank of individual wooden boxes mounted beside the front desk and looked inside hers, hoping to see the familiar long, tan envelope, it wasn't there.

As the days passed into a week, then into nine days, her hopes faded. On the tenth day, she was so discouraged that she had decided not to look in her message box. But as she was passing it, she did glance over to see a tan envelope sticking out of the open end of her box. A shock of adrenaline ran from the top of her head down to the soles of her feet as she pretended to remain calm as she pulled out Jed's letter. Then, not being able to contain her anxiety any longer, she tore open the letter and began to read right there in the lobby.

Her happy smile quickly turned to a frown, however. And the more she read, the deeper the frown grew.

And Caitlin, I know you'll understand why I won't be coming to Virginia for the Christmas holidays as we'd planned. I don't see how I can with my father being so sick. I know there's not a lot that has to be done around the ranch during winter. But, still, I can't leave Melanie alone to cope with any emergency that might come up.

Eve's been a real friend through all this and has promised to do whatever she can to help. She's good on a horse, as you know, and can handle a downed steer as well as any ranch hand.

Perhaps I can visit you during spring break. I don't know. I guess the only thing to do is to wait and see.

I'm sorry I forgot your birthday. I'll make it up to you, honest. But I'm sure you can understand, what with all that's been going on with me, and with my father's illness. All I can hope is that is doesn't turn out to be anything too serious.

As always,
Jed

Oh, hah! Caitlin wanted to scream. *His father's illness! Hah!* Who did Jed think he was kidding? It was just an excuse. If Jed really wanted to come for Christmas, Melanie would be able to cope. After all, what did they have hired hands for, anyway? And Eve! Jed made it sound as if he and Eve were going to single-handedly run the ranch. Well, the only thing that letter told her was that he preferred Eve's company during Christmas break to hers. With a cold fury, Caitlin tore the letter into a hundred tiny pieces and threw them in the nearest wastebasket. She could read between the lines: Jed just wanted to stay in Montana and play house with Eve. Well, she would show him!

Going to her room, she sat down and wrote the shortest letter she'd ever written to Jed.

Dear Jed,
Of course I understand your reasons for not wanting to come East. And maybe it's for the best. We both seem to be so busy with our separate lives.

Caitlin

Jed's reaction was not long in coming. It came on Saturday as a phone call.

Caitlin, along with Hal, Louise, and Julian, had planned to attend the big football game together on that Saturday before Thanksgiving. The game against Carleton Hill's most bitter rival, the State College Bears, was the highlight of the football season. And Carleton Hill was favored to win. Afterward, the four had planned to go to dinner at Roberto's. It was meant to be a friendly foursome, not an actual double date.

But on Friday Louise received a call from her mother asking her to come home because she had broken her wrist and needed Louise's help. As soon as she hung up the phone, Louise told Caitlin.

"Listen, I hate to leave you with both guys. Why don't you call Ginny and see if she'd like to go."

When Caitlin called her a few minutes later, Ginny sounded delighted with the invitation, even though it was last minute.

Caitlin was waiting in the lobby when Ginny arrived the next morning. As the door opened, Caitlin had to stare for a long moment before she was really sure it was her friend.

"Ginny!" she gasped as her old roommate

came up to her. "You look fabulous! What have you done to yourself?"

"Do you like it?" Laughing, Ginny pivoted in front of Caitlin. "It's the new me."

"Well, I love your hair. And that sweater—it's so great on you. I just can't remember ever seeing you wear anything like it before."

"I know, I know." Ginny smiled, suddenly feeling a little self-conscious. "But I thought it was time for a change. My look was getting so predictable that I couldn't stand it anymore." Looking down, she pulled out the front of her oversize sweater, as if to reaffirm that she was actually wearing the bulky purple knit. "Do you really like it? I think it's Italian, but you know designers better than I do." With a happy shrug, she let go of the sweater, and the hem of it dropped back down to her hips. She was also wearing heathery purple wool pants and simple black flats. "I'm so used to everything coming from Lands' End, or L. L. Bean. Of course, the second I put my coat back on, it'll be hidden."

"But there's still your new haircut. I definitely like it cut that way." Caitlin tipped her head one way, then back the other as she studied Ginny's feathery new hairstyle. "It makes you look kind of pixieish. When did you get it cut?"

"Uh—right after the last time I was here." Ginny blushed. *Right after I met Julian Stokes*, she thought.

Caitlin misinterpreted her friend's blush. "Ginny! You've got a new boyfriend, right?" Suddenly she remembered Win. "It's not on the rebound from Win, is it?" she asked with concern.

"Caitlin, honestly!" Ginny blushed even more. "There's no one new. I swear."

"Well, all right." Caitlin gave her a skeptical look. "It is cold out today, so maybe that's why your cheeks are so red. But—" she stopped abruptly. "Oh, look, there are the guys now." She smiled at Ginny. "Ready to have a great time this afternoon?"

"Ready!" Ginny smiled back.

"Oh, I still don't believe that last touchdown," Caitlin said, laughing as she and Hal walked back through the front door of the dorm several hours later.

"I don't either," Hal agreed. With that humongous pileup, I wasn't sure they'd find Darrell in one piece at the bottom."

"But we won!"

"I know. Isn't that the greatest?" On impulse, Hal picked Caitlin up and swung her around.

Julian and Ginny came in a second later. Julian had accompanied Ginny to where her car was parked to make sure it hadn't been ticketed by the campus police for being parked in the visitors' lot all day.

They walked up to Hal and Caitlin as Hal was putting Caitlin down. The girl at the front desk called to Caitlin.

"Oh, Caitlin—great. You're here. There's a long-distance call for you on the house phone. Whoever it is said he'd been trying to reach you. He was just going to leave a message. You can take the call on the downstairs extension if you want."

"A phone call? For me?" Caitlin repeated. "Thanks, I will take it down here." With an apprehensive look at Ginny, she mouthed, "Jed!" Then she looked at the two boys. "Excuse me. I won't be long."

When Caitlin walked back toward them a few minutes later, the three fell silent. They all knew that something was wrong.

The first thing Julian noticed was the paleness of Caitlin's skin, highlighted by two bright spots of color that burned high on her cheeks.

Caitlin excused herself from going out to dinner with them. She said she hoped they would understand. It had been a long and tiring day, and she just wanted to lie down for a while.

The three stood, frozen, watching as she turned, walked toward the elevator, and got on. The elevator doors closed.

Suddenly Ginny sprang into action. "Wait here," she told Hal and Julian as she headed toward the stairs. "I'll be right back."

15

Ginny raced up the stairs, two at a time. She saw Caitlin at the other end of the third-floor hall. "Caitlin—Caitlin!" Ginny called. "Wait a minute!" She raced down the hall after her friend. "I want to talk to you."

"But I already told you that I don't want to talk, Ginny," Caitlin called back over her shoulder. "Why don't you go out with the guys and have dinner? I want to be alone for a while." Caitlin pushed the door of her room open and went in.

"Caitlin—" Ginny pushed in after her. "I can't just go off and leave you like this. I want to know if you're okay. Please, can't we talk?"

Caitlin had collapsed onto the bed. "Please go, Ginny," she pleaded. "Honestly, I just want to be alone. Don't you understand? I don't want to—" She stopped, no longer able to speak. A sob tore from her throat, and she buried her face in her hands.

"Caitlin! Oh, Caitlin." Ginny sank down onto the bed beside Caitlin. "Whatever it is, I'm sure it's not as bad as you think." She stroked Caitlin's shoulder, trying to make her feel better. She waited until her friend's sobs grew quieter.

"It—it's Jed," Caitlin finally managed to get out. "It's over. This time it's really over between us." Caitlin gave a soft little hiccup and sat up. Her face was swollen from weeping.

"Tell me what happened?" Ginny prodded gently.

"Well, Jed didn't send a letter until ten days after my birthday. He had forgotten it."

"I don't believe it!"

"Believe it!" Caitlin said unhappily. "And in the same letter he said he wouldn't be coming to Virginia for Christmas break because his father's sick. But it's so easy to see through his excuse. It's so obvious, Ginny."

"Obvious?"

"Yes. Don't you see? He wants to stay there and be with Eve. So"—Caitlin gave a ragged sigh—"I wrote back. And, well, I suppose it really wasn't a very nice letter."

"Well, my God! It shouldn't have been. I mean, I wouldn't have written him at all. I would have called him right then and told him exactly what I thought of him."

"Ginny, that's exactly what he did to me—just now. He was so cold. He said it was obvious that

158

I didn't want to go out with him anymore."
Caitlin swallowed hard. "I wanted to tell him
how wrong he was, but I just couldn't bring
myself to do it. So I ended up being cold to him,
too. Then it just got worse and worse and worse.
I don't remember hanging up, Ginny. I don't
even remember if I said goodbye to him."

"Caitlin, listen to me. I think you did the right
thing. Jed has been acting like a total jerk. And
you're better off without him." She frowned,
thinking. "There are so many guys right here on
campus. Look at Hal, for instance. I was watching you two today. You were having a great time
together. And he's every bit as cute as Jed."

"Hal's really nice. But he just can't compare to
Jed."

"Well, maybe not. But he's here, and Jed's a
long way away."

"Don't I know it!" Caitlin nodded jerkily.
"That's been the whole problem. If Jed hadn't
given in to what his father wanted, he'd be here
right now. And none of this would have happened."

"Caitlin, you don't know that. Maybe you
would have broken up even if he'd come to
Carleton Hill. You know, I never did think Jed fit
in here in the East. There was always too much
cowboy in him."

Caitlin started to cry again. "I'm sorry," Ginny
apologized, realizing that all she had done was

bring up one of the things that Caitlin found so fascinating about Jed.

"No, no!" Caitlin shook her head as a tear slid down her cheek. "I really—I really appreciate your trying to comfort me. You're a terrific friend, Ginny. Even though I don't agree with what you've just said about Jed, I know why you said it." Reaching over, she touched Ginny's arm. "But, honest, right now I just want to be by myself. Okay? Louise won't be back until tomorrow, and that means I can be all alone in the room and do some thinking. Do you mind going back to school tonight?"

"No, not if that's what you really want." Ginny hesitated, then stood up. But she turned and gazed down at Caitlin. "Are you positive you're going to be all right here alone? I mean, you're not going to just sit and cry, are you?"

"Don't be silly." Caitlin gave her a weak smile. "You know me better than that."

"Yeah, I guess I do." Ginny moved toward the door. "What do you want me to tell Hal? He's waiting downstairs with Julian."

"Oh, I don't know." Caitlin sighed. "I've already apologized."

"I suppose you could call it that," Ginny said kindly. "Well, then I guess I'll just say goodbye."

"Are you still going to go out to dinner with them?"

"I might. I'll see what happens when I get

back downstairs. Anyway, you take care of yourself. I'm going to call you sometime tomorrow to check and see how you are. All right?"

"All right." Caitlin gave her a shaky smile. "And thanks, Ginny. You're such a good friend."

"And you'll always be my best friend," Ginny said.

She closed the door quietly behind her as she left the room.

Julian and Hal were waiting for her. Hal looked uncomfortable, but Ginny didn't know why exactly. She guessed he wanted to get out of going to dinner with Julian and her.

Julian looked very concerned. Ginny smiled at him.

"Caitlin's fine. She was a bit upset by the phone call she received. And she really does send her apologies, but she'd rather stay in than go to dinner as we'd planned."

"Oh!" Hal looked visibly relieved. "Well, I'm glad it's not anything really serious. I think in that case, I'll just go home. Maybe I'll give her a call tomorrow—you know, to see how she is." He backed away a couple of steps. Then, as if belatedly realizing they were supposed to be going to dinner together, he looked from Ginny, to Julian, and back to Ginny again. "Are you two still going out to eat?"

"Ah—ummm—" Ginny hesitated, embarrassed.

"Yes, I believe we are," Julian said, coming to her rescue with a decisive answer.

"Hey, great!" Hal backed away a few more steps. "I'm sure you'll enjoy it more if I'm not along—you know, fifth wheel, and all that."

As soon as he'd left, Ginny turned toward Julian. Shyly, she said, "You really don't have to take me to dinner. I've had a great time today. But it wasn't as if it were a real date or anything."

"Well, I'll tell you what," Julian said, smiling his slow, winning smile. "Why don't we make it one—for dinner, anyway."

"Well, all right." Ginny found she was automatically returning his smile. "I'd love to."

"Wonderful." Julian took her arm. "But since it will be only the two of us, perhaps we shouldn't go to Roberto's. Tell me, do you like French food?"

"I love French food," Ginny replied, telling herself that she would eat a bucket of slimy snails in garlic butter if it meant having dinner alone with Julian.

After a truly delicious meal, one that did not feature a single snail, Julian and Ginny sat, enjoying their coffee. Looking across the table at

Julian, Ginny noticed that the flickering candle in the low bowl between them lit tiny fires in the depths of Julian's normally cool gray eyes.

All through dinner he insisted on talking only about her, asking her questions about her childhood, favorite movies, books, music—and, of course, about horses.

Now, taking her first sip of the strong, aromatic coffee, she realized she had learned very little about him. There was something he said earlier that made her think he had grown up somewhere near Washington, D.C. Yet, he had a slight accent. She decided to ask him about it. "Where are you—"

"That phone call Caitlin received tonight—it was from Jed, wasn't it?" Julian deftly changed the subject to Caitlin.

Ginny nodded. "Yes. How did you guess?"

"Well, I know that she hasn't been happy lately—and that the reason has been her problems with Jed. I only needed to put one and one together to come up with a pretty miserable two." He shook his head. "I'm afraid I don't think Jed is very good for her."

"Neither do I," Ginny agreed readily. "In fact, that's exactly what I told her when I went up to see her before we left."

"What did Caitlin say?"

"She blames everything that's happened between them on the fact that they're apart. I thought so, too, for a while. But I've watched Caitlin and Jed go through trouble before, and he's never been this selfish. This time, I think it's because they're just not right for each other—they're from two different worlds. Do you know what I mean?"

"Yes," Julian lowered his eyes, concealing the expression in them from her. "I know very well what you mean." Picking up his spoon, he began to stir his black coffee. The details of the next phase of his plan to hurt Caitlin Ryan went through his head. Only this time, he would make use of his new friendship with Ginny. She could help quite a bit.

When he looked up again, his expression had changed. He had the look of someone who is about to give someone else a present and is hoping that person will like it. "Ginny, I want to ask you something."

"What?" Ginny asked as she held her breath.

"We've had so much fun together this afternoon and this evening, I wonder—I wonder if you'd like to go to Fort Lauderdale for part of winter break with me?"

"Florida?" A tiny thrill went racing through her. But an instant later she stopped to consider what he'd said. Suddenly a wave of anger and outrage flooded over her. Just who did he think he was? Worse, what kind of girl did he think she was?

When Julian saw the shock on her face, he realized how she was taking his invitation. He also realized that he should have been more subtle. Quickly putting his spoon down, he reached across the table and touched her hand lightly. "Oh, please, I hope you haven't misunderstood me and jumped to the wrong conclusion. See, there's a student discount tour." He gave a self-deprecating laugh. "I'm afraid that's the only kind of trip I'll be able to afford for the next several years, as long as I'm a medical student."

"Oh." That was different, Ginny thought. They would be with a lot of students, yet she would have time to get to know Julian better. But she knew she would have to turn him down because her parents would never approve. But now he was talking about—what *was* he talking about? She listened as he went on.

"The sand, the sun, and tropical waters of the Atlantic. It should be a lot of fun. A real break from winter and studying."

Ginny smiled. "It does sound like fun."

"And I have another marvelous idea." He touched her hand again. "What would you think about asking Caitlin to go along, too?"

"Great," Ginny said. "Knowing that Caitlin's going, too, is probably the only reason my parents will let me go."

16

$\backsim$

"Come on, Caitlin, please say you'll go!" Ginny asked urgently over the phone. "Please!"

"Sorry, Ginny, I can't."

"Caitlin, just think about it for a minute. Think about lying on the golden beaches or swimming in the ocean, sailing in one of those boats on pontoons, or maybe riding a motor scooter along a palm-lined road, walking along the edge of the surf under the starry skies—"

"Stop!" Caitlin laughed in spite of the miserable way she was feeling. "Ginny, you sound just like a travel brochure."

"All right, then look at it another way." Ginny's voice was persuasive. "By then, you'll need a break from your studies. And, who knows, maybe you'll meet some really handsome guy down there."

"Ginny"— Caitlin's voice had a warning edge to it—"this is not the time to talk to me about guys."

"Then just think about the studies part. You'll come back from Florida all tan and healthy and ready to plunge right into second semester." Ginny paused. "Besides, Caitlin, if you don't go, it means I can't go."

"Why? How come?"

"I talked to my parents late last night. They agreed that the trip could be one of my Christmas presents, but only if you're going, too. They don't want me going alone."

"Honestly, Ginny! You'd hardly be alone. It's one of those student discount trips. There are bound to be at least fifty other kids going down with you."

"As far as my parents are concerned, they'll just be fifty strangers. Nope. If you don't go, I can't either."

"I'm really sorry, Ginny," Caitlin said softly. "But the last thing I want to think about right now is going to Florida for part of winter break. I don't even think I'll feel like leaving my dorm room for the next month."

"But that's just about how far away the trip is," Ginny persisted.

"Besides," Caitlin went on as if she hadn't heard Ginny speak, "I really have to spend some time at Ryan Acres with my grandmother. I haven't been home once this term. And there's my father, too. I'd like to spend some time with him."

167

"Thanksgiving is this week. You'll see everyone for a few days. And you'll spend Christmas at home. The trip is after Christmas."

Caitlin replied in a firm, yet friendly voice. "I said no. I don't want to go, okay? That's final."

"You're positive?"

"I'm positive!"

"Well, if you change your mind"—Ginny sounded very disappointed—"you'll call me right away, won't you?"

"Yes." Caitlin touched the mouthpiece lightly with her finger as if to reassure Ginny that she wasn't upset with her. "I promise. If I change my mind, I'll let you know immediately. But please, Ginny, don't hold your breath."

With a heavy sigh, Caitlin replaced the receiver and went back to her studies. Her Cliff Notes for Thomas Hardy's *The Return of the Native* were still open to the page she had been reading, and Caitlin tried to pick up where she'd left off. But what was the use? She couldn't concentrate.

She had read the book, so it shouldn't have been difficult to answer the questions Dr. Longwood had handed out about the author's philosophy of love versus the Victorian morality of the times. But, try as she might, she couldn't form even one clear sentence. Each time she wrote the word "love," her mind immediately filled with a picture of Jed declaring his undying love for her.

Finally, she threw down the pen and got to her feet.

She paced the length of the room, then back again. It was too quiet. That was the problem. She switched on the radio and found her favorite music station. The DJ was just finishing the half-hour newsbreak. "And the time is now nine thirty-one," he announced. Then a song came on. She almost couldn't believe it. It was a love song she and Jed had danced to at a party at his ranch. She flicked off the radio.

She walked to the stereo. Her hand paused over a cassette. No, there were too many memories there, too. Turning, she went to the window and looked out. Her third-floor window overlooked the edge of the campus and part of a parking lot. If she leaned against the glass and looked to her right, she could see fraternity row and her sorority house. Maybe she should go over there? But, no, it was still too early. Everyone usually slept in on Sundays. As a rule, she did, too.

So why am I awake? Caitlin asked herself. There had been the call from Ginny, who was a notorious early riser, but that wasn't it. She had been awake even before the sun came up. And she had lain there for a long time, thinking. Finally realizing she was not going to get back to sleep, she had gotten out of bed, dressed, and gone down to the lobby to get a cup of coffee from the vending machine. She brought it and an apple back to her room, deciding she might as well study.

She glanced over at her desk. Well, a fat lot of work she had managed to get done. Wrapping her arms across her chest, she tucked her hands under her upper arms. She'd told Ginny that all she wanted to do was stay in her room. Yet, there she was, about to go crazy because she didn't want to be alone for one more minute.

A movement on the walk down below caught her eye. She looked. It was a boy and girl jogging together. There was something about the boy that reminded her of Hal. She squinted, trying to see him better. It wasn't Hal. The boy had brown hair, not blond.

Hal! She felt bad about the way she had deserted him the previous evening. It hadn't been nice. But she couldn't help it. Jed's phone call had turned her into a positive wreck. *Jed! Forget Jed*, she told herself firmly. *Think about Hal.*

She remembered he'd said something during halftime at the game the day before—something about how they weren't getting in enough tennis lately. She wondered if he would be up so early. And if he was, if they could get a court on a Sunday morning on such short notice. *Sure they'll have one*, Caitlin told herself. They would probably have to wait a little bit for it, but so what? They could talk. She felt like talking. She felt like talking a lot—about anything. It didn't really matter. Anything to make her forget Jed. And she would, she vowed. "I hate him," she said softly.

"Oh, hi, Caitlin!" Louise glanced up from where she sat cross-legged on the floor. Open books were spread out around her as she tried to figure out a chemistry assignment.

"Hi!" Caitlin answered, a bit breathlessly. "The elevator's been doing its sticking number again, so I had to run up the stairs. Don't worry." She waved at Louise. "I won't be long. I'm only here to change. Then I'm going out again."

"Boy!" Louise shook her head, almost in awe. "When you decide to stop moping around, you don't fool around! It's only been about two and a half weeks since you broke up with Jed, and you've been out on at least fourteen dates. I may have lost count. Where are you going this time?" Leaning forward, she watched as Caitlin went into action.

"Dinner with Tony Wishorn," Caitlin said breezily as she shrugged out of her lemon yellow sweats and walked barefoot to her dresser. She pulled on a pair of panty hose, then padded over to the closet. "It's a good thing I decided to take a shower at the gym after my tennis game with Hal," she said over her shoulder. "On my way up the stairs, I ran into Kathy from down the hall. She told me that the ones in the dorm are backed up again."

"Oh, no," Louise moaned. "And I wanted to take a shower tonight."

"Well, try the gym," Caitlin suggested as she pulled a white knit dress from its hanger and slipped it over her head. "The locker room's almost deserted."

"Maybe I will," Louise replied, not moving. She was mesmerized by Caitlin's quick-change act.

The dress Caitlin had put on hung straight from her shoulders. She added a dark green leather belt, cinching it only tight enough to emphasize her slim waist. Then she stepped into a pair of pointed-toed red and dark green heels and walked back to the dresser, where she rummaged through the drawers until she came up with a green-and-red print silk scarf. Artfully, she began to wind it around her neck. "Oh, and we're going to a concert at the music school afterward," she said, fastening the scarf with the gold pin her father had sent. "Some famous cellist. I have no idea what his name is." She shook her head as she unclasped the clip that held her hair back from her face. "I'm pretty good on pianists and violinists, but when it comes to any other instruments, I'm lost." Picking up a brush, she vigorously attacked her hair, quickly taming it so that it lay sleek and shining around her shoulders. "But Tony says this cellist is good, and I trust him. Since he's a music major."

"Uh-huh." Louise nodded. "You know, Caitlin, one of these days you've got to wind down a little. If I didn't know better, I'd swear you were high on something. You hardly ever sleep anymore. Haven't you got a big art history assignment due the day after tomorrow? Last time I heard, you hadn't even started it."

"Don't worry, Louise," Caitlin assured her as she crossed once more to the closet, this time to pull out a coat. "That's all taken care of. Stan Giles has promised to help me with it. It's not so much a matter of writing as just spending a couple of hours in the library putting together prints from the archives in the basement. We're going to do it tomorrow afternoon." She slipped her arms into the coat.

"Julian asked about you," Louise mentioned casually.

"Oh, really!"

"Yes. He's worried about you. I mean about the way you're running yourself into the ground. I told him how you're not sleeping, and you're not really eating. You look like you've lost at least five pounds in the last week."

"Well, if I have, then it's probably because I needed to," Caitlin said defensively.

"That's not true," Louise said flatly.

"Look, just tell Julian thank you." Caitlin picked up her purse and pulled the collar of her coat up so that it protected her from the chilly wind. "But I don't think I need his advice."

"Do you honestly want me to tell Julian that?" Louise inquired in a sweet voice. "It doesn't sound like a very good answer to give to someone who really cares about you."

"Oh!" Realizing the truth of what her roommate had just said, Caitlin shook her head. "Of course you're right, Louise. How absolutely thoughtless of me. I do appreciate the fact that he cares. Please tell him that for me. But also tell him that I'm just fine." She smiled. "Look, it's the holiday season. And you go out partying, too!"

"But not nearly so much as you do, Caitlin," Louise reminded her. And wasn't that the unhappy truth, she thought. As she glanced over at Caitlin looking so beautiful, a bitter taste rose to the back of Louise's throat. If this was what Julian had meant when he had said he would take care of Caitlin, then Louise wished he would do the same for her. She'd been trying to get Tony Wishorn to ask her out ever since she'd first met him in music appreciation at the beginning of her freshman year. "Look, Caitlin, the fact is that we both care about what happens to you."

"And I love you for that," Caitlin replied with honest emotion. "That's why I count you and Julian among my dearest friends. But, please, don't worry." She paused, then gaily added, "I'm having the time of my life. And speaking of time. I'd better run. I don't want to keep Tony waiting."

Actually, Caitlin wasn't having all that wonderful a time. It was as though she were attempting to convince herself, by dancing from one boy to the next, that she was having fun. And if she moved fast enough, perhaps she'd be able to forget about Jed, if only for a little while.

Still, the pain of losing him was never far from her mind. She was thankful when the term finally ended and she could go home to Ryan Acres for Christmas. Even though her home wasn't a model of family togetherness, at least she would be able to relax and unwind.

17

"'Sleep in heavenly peace. . . .'" The voices of the carolers faded softly in the crisp night air.

Caitlin, dressed in a long velvet skirt of deep burgundy and a high-necked white lace blouse, stood beside her grandmother in the open doorway of the mansion. As always, she was moved by the classic tableau the group of youngsters made, all very Charles Dickens-like, with their colorful mufflers and knitted hats and mittens.

As they finished the final line from "Silent Night," she moved aside so that Rollins could come through the door, bearing a large silver tray that held steaming mugs of hot apple cider and Mrs. Crowley's homemade doughnuts, which the cook had baked in anticipation of the visit by the youngsters. It was a tradition for the young people of the town to be driven from estate to estate and herald in Christmas Eve with carols.

Caitlin adored tradition. And that night was

the most tradition filled of all. Because the dining room was so large, a small table had been set up in the study for Christmas Eve dinner. It had been covered with a double cloth of green velvet and white Irish linen and set with the family's gold-rimmed plates and gold-plated flat-ware. A low centerpiece of holly and white candles graced the middle of the table. A dinner of roast beef and Yorkshire pudding would be served, and for dessert, Rollins would come in bearing a dramatic, flaming plum pudding.

Then afterward, they would go into the living room where the ceiling-high tree awaited them.

Caitlin turned to follow her grandmother back into the house after the caroling. Inhaling the pungent aroma of the Christmas tree, as well as the sprigs of pine that were twined around the banister and draped over every mantelpiece, she told herself that she wouldn't let anything ruin that special night, not even Colin.

But when she walked into the study and saw him standing by the fire, the fingers of his right hand thrust casually into the pocket of his vest, the other holding a cigar, the chokingly rich smoke of which nearly overwhelmed the fragrance of the pine, she felt her resolve wavering.

Colin played the part of the perfect gentleman, seating her grandmother first, then Caitlin, at the beautifully laid table.

But then the roast was brought in. Instead of

Rollins carving it, as he had always done, Colin took charge of the antique bone-handled knife and fork. It was nearly too much for Caitlin. For the rest of the meal she couldn't get the sight of Colin standing there carving, out of her mind. He was acting as if he were the host and she the guest. She barely tasted the succulent beef and dumplinglike Yorkshire pudding Mrs. Crowley had baked. And the plum pudding was like soggy cardboard in her mouth.

For the five days that Caitlin had been home at Ryan Acres, the only time she really felt free of Colin's presence—even though he wasn't actually there quite that much—was when she went to her room or out riding. And what was worse was that her grandmother didn't seem capable of uttering a single sentence without bringing Colin's name into the conversation. "Colin has done this . . . Colin has done that . . . Colin thinks this . . ." It was driving Caitlin crazy.

With dinner over at last, they adjourned to the living room. The tree, which had been hand-picked by Mrs. Ryan behind the estate, was lighted with hundreds of crystal-white lights that reflected mirrorlike prisms on the hand-made, gold-and-white ornaments—so numerous that they almost hid the branches from sight.

In years past Caitlin had enjoyed this part of the evening best—not so much for the presents that would be opened as for the time of sharing with her grandmother.

This year it was as though Colin was purposefully separating them. Leading her grandmother to a chair, he sat her down, making sure she was comfortable. A brief thought flitted through Caitlin's mind. Her grandmother looked very much the queen, in her floor-length, silver-gray velvet hostess gown, the same color as her elegantly done hair. Did Colin picture himself her prince consort?

"Go ahead, Caitlin, open your presents," he told her. Walking over to a table on which sat a row of crystal decanters, he picked up the one holding the Napoleon brandy and poured out two snifters of the amber liquid. Returning to Regina Ryan's side, he handed her one, then sat down on a nearby chair and prepared to watch as Caitlin unwrapped the beautiful packages piled high beneath the lower branches of the tree.

Later, lying in bed, Caitlin decided that with that one single action, Colin had made her feel as if she were once again a little girl. She may as well have been dressed in a party dress and black patent leather shoes, waiting breathlessly to see how many dolls she would receive. As for the presents that night, she couldn't recall a single one clearly.

Well, tomorrow will be better, she promised

herself, turning and pulling the covers up to her chin. Tomorrow *would* be better, because her father would be coming to spend Christmas with her.

"Father! Oh, Father!" Running to him as he stood in the doorway of the mansion, Caitlin threw her arms around his neck, then pressed her cheek against his, which was cold from the outdoors. She closed her eyes and inhaled the spiciness of his expensive cologne. "I've missed you so very, very much."

"And I've missed you, too, kitten." Dr. Westlake chuckled warmly. Then he pulled away from her embrace to hold her at arm's length so he could take a good look at her. His clear blue eyes twinkled. "Let's see how much you've changed since I last saw you."

"Gordon, honestly!" Regina Ryan spoke from where she stood several feet away. "Will you please come all the way into the house so that Rollins can close the door. You're not only allowing the heat to escape, but you've left poor Nicole standing out there on the steps."

"Oh, Nicole, dear. I'm so sorry," he said, ushering the tall blond inside.

"Sorry, Regina," Dr. Westlake apologized with just the right amount of deference required for politeness. Moving away from Caitlin in order to take Nicole's arm, he led her forward.

"Hello, Caitlin," the sophisticated woman said. She was carrying a medium-sized package wrapped in gold-flocked foil.

"Hello, Nicole," Caitlin replied. She could not help but notice the platinum-and-diamond earrings in Nicole's ears, and her gaze went right to them.

Nicole saw her look and reached a graceful hand up to touch one. "A Christmas present from Gordon." She smiled sweetly. "And this is for you." She handed Caitlin the package. "From him."

"Thank you," Caitlin said, accepting the present.

"Rollins, take their coats, please," Mrs. Ryan directed, in charge again.

The group stood waiting, while the butler took Nicole's street-length, silver fox coat and Dr. Westlake's overcoat. Then they all went into the living room.

"And I have presents for you, too," Caitlin said. Going over to the tree and reaching under it, she pulled out two tastefully wrapped packages. She handed one to Nicole; the other she put into her father's hands. "I hope you like it," she said softly. "The minute I saw it, I knew it was the right present for you."

"I know I'll love it." He gestured with his

hand at the gift that Caitlin had put down on a chair in order to retrieve the presents from under the tree. "But why don't you open yours first?"

"Oh, no," Caitlin said eagerly. "I don't think I can wait another second. I'm dying to see if you like what I got you."

Dr. Westlake chuckled. "All right. I'll open mine before you open yours. But first, I think we should let Nicole open the one you gave her." He turned his gaze on Nicole, who was now sitting in a graceful pose on the edge of one of the sofas.

"It was thoughtful of you to get me a present," Nicole simpered. "I'm afraid I didn't get one for you. How thoughtless of me."

"But you did spend time and effort helping me pick out the present for Caitlin," Dr. Westlake countered. "Which really makes it from you as much as from me."

"Well, if that's the way you feel, Gordon. . . ." Nicole flashed him a dazzling smile. Then she admitted a little too modestly, "I did have to phone Paris three times to make sure it would arrive here in time."

"I'm afraid my gift is just a little something I found in one of the boutiques near school," Caitlin said, feeling her breathing begin to quicken as her dislike of Nicole began to rise to the surface. *Calm. Stay calm*, she firmly told herself, not wanting to ruin the day.

"Oh, but I'm certain you did your best, dear," Nicole said. "It's not your fault that you couldn't go somewhere where there was decent shopping." Tearing the pink and silver paper away from the small box, she opened the top and looked in. "Ohh." She raised a delicate eyebrow. "How quaint." Then she held up the object for everyone to see. "A pillbox."

"That's lovely, Caitlin," Dr. Westlake exclaimed. "Isn't that cloisonné?"

"Yes." Caitlin nodded, smiling. "When I saw it, I knew it was just perfect for Nicole." *That's right*, she thought, continuing to smile. *A pillbox for a real pill.*

"Well, now you open yours, Gordon." With a careless gesture, Nicole put the pillbox down on the sofa beside her. It would have rolled off if Colin hadn't sprung forward and deftly caught it. He quietly placed it on a nearby end table.

"Yes, I can hardly wait," Dr. Westlake said happily as he opened the gift.

"Uh—what is it, Gordon?" Nicole sat forward and craned her neck. "I can't tell from here."

"It's a carving," Dr. Westlake explained. "Of a tired doctor." He grinned. "I bet he's just come from spending the night helping a new baby come into the world."

"Looks rather crude to me," Nicole observed.

183

"That's part of its charm," Caitlin retorted. "And that's just what it is, Father, a carving done by one of the mountain men in West Virginia."

Nicole shrugged. "Well, dear, we know you don't have a lot of time to shop."

"I don't care if I could have had the time to go to Washington, I still would have picked out that carving," Caitlin answered.

"Caitlin!" Colin broke in. "You still haven't opened your present yet. We'd love to see what it is."

"Oh, yes, do open it," Nicole said. "I think you'll really like it. It's definitely you."

Caitlin slowly began to open the elaborately wrapped package. She knew, before she even opened it, that she was going to hate it. Her father hadn't picked it out—Nicole had. What would she find inside? Would she be able to cover up her true feelings if whatever it was really was as awful as she feared it might be? She didn't want to hurt her father. But, oh, how could he have let Nicole pick out her Christmas present? It wasn't like him to do something like that.

The paper was off. She lifted the lid from the box. Oh, God! It was more than awful. It was horrible! Slowly she lifted what had to be a sweater into the light of the room. Yes, that's what it was—a sweater. But where would she ever wear it? It looked as though a collection of every piece of glitzy, tasteless decoration ever designed—beads, sequins, feathers—had been thrown helter-skelter at it and had stuck. This was even worse, in a way than the lynx coat. At least, she had been able to let Colin know how she felt. This time the present was supposed to be from someone who really loved her, who really cared. Her father.

"Don't you just love it?" Nicole asked. There was a thrill in her voice.

Caitlin could only stare at her in stunned silence for several seconds. Then what came out of her mouth was a completely honest answer. "No, Nicole. I hate it!"

"Caitlin!" Her grandmother gasped in embarrassment.

"Really, Caitlin. You don't mean that, do you?" Colin's tone was diplomatic.

"Caitlin!" Dr. Westlake spoke with barely controlled anger. "I can't believe my ears. I can't believe a daughter of mine would say something like that. I want you to apologize to Nicole immediately."

"I'm sorry, but I'm only being truthful," Caitlin responded. "You gave me such beautiful gifts for my birthday. Father, how could you have let her pick out my present?"

"What has that got to do with your bad manners?"

"I—I just want to know."

"And I want you to apologize."

"You don't understand!" she accused him.

"You're damned right I don't understand!"

"I thought you loved me. I picked out my present for you because I love you. Nicole—"

They were suddenly interrupted by Rollins coming into the room.

"Yes, Rollins?" Mrs. Ryan addressed him.

"I'm terribly sorry to disturb you, ma'am. But there's a phone call for Miss Ryan."

"Tell them she'll call back. She can't possibly come to the phone right now."

"Who is the phone call from, Rollins?" Caitlin spoke up.

"Jed Michaels, Miss Ryan."

"I'll take it." Caitlin rose and walked quickly from the room, without looking back.

Going into the library, she picked up the extension there. "Jed?"

"Caitlin?" The wire crackled.

"This is a terrible connection. Let me call you back."

"Uh—well, I just called to wish you a Merry Christmas."

"Yes well, let me call you back, Jed. I can barely hear you."

"Oh—well, all right. Do you have a pencil? I'll give you the phone number."

"Why? I know the number at the ranch by

heart." She hesitated. "Don't tell me you're at school! Not on Christmas."

"No, that's not where I am. Do you have a pencil?"

"Jed! Where are you?"

"There was a snowstorm—"

"Where are you?"

"I'm at the Towerses' ranch."

"You're at Eve's house?"

"Yes. I came over to bring a present—"

"A present for Eve! You sent me a crummy card, and you're giving Eve a present?" Caitlin saw little white spots dancing in front of her eyes. "I don't believe it!"

"Let me explain—"

"No! No, no, no! I will not let you explain. There is nothing to explain. A present is a present. And a crummy card is a crummy card. Goodbye, Jed!" She slammed down the receiver.

It took at least three minutes for Caitlin to get her breathing back to normal. When she did, she reached for the phone again. Picking up the receiver, she dialed a familiar number. It rang three times before someone answered.

"Hello."

"Ginny? This is Caitlin. Do you still want to go to Florida?"

"Why—yes!" Ginny stuttered. "Of—of course I do."

"Good. Because I've changed my mind. And I want to leave as soon as we can get reservations. The student discount will be out, obviously. We'll just have to fly down on our own."

"Sure. Terrific." There was a pause. "Aren't you even going to say Merry Christmas?"

"Merry Christmas, Ginny."

18

"I don't believe the heat." Ginny sighed and wiped her forehead for the third time in a matter of minutes. "I'm not sure I'm glad I came."

They were waiting outside the terminal for a cab to take them to Fort Lauderdale and their hotel.

"I admit it is a little muggy," Caitlin said. "But you should have dressed for the change. What are you doing in a sweater?"

"Well, it was so cold in Virginia, I just didn't think."

"Don't worry." Caitlin smiled sympathetically. "The second we get to the hotel you can put on a bathing suit and go down and flop on the beach."

"That's exactly what I'm going to do. I want to get a tan for the party tonight."

Caitlin nodded knowingly. "I think I'd better keep an eye on you. You sound more like you're heading for a sunburn."

Despite the temperature change and the tiring flight south to Florida, Caitlin was feeling pretty good. And she was definitely in the mood to go to a party, she told herself as they climbed into a taxi.

As she looked through the window—fascinated by the tropical landscape and the light, which was so much brighter than that in Virginia—she thought back a few days, to when she had hung up on Jed.

When she had received a Christmas card from him two days after coming home, she thought, perhaps, that the card was a sign that he wanted to make up. True, he had only signed it "Jed." But the printed message had read, "Christmas is Love." So, how else was she supposed to interpret it?

But then when he had called her from Eve's and told her he'd brought Eve a present. . . . Well, that was definitely the bitter end! There was no going back now. Not ever!

Perhaps it was the combination of anger she had built up toward Colin and Nicole in addition to that for Jed that made her feel the way she was feeling right then. Whatever it was, it was as if someone had flipped a switch to "on" that had been in the "off" position for far too long. Because the old, flirtatious Caitlin was back. Back to stay!

* * *

Julian sat in the lobby of the hotel, waiting for Caitlin to arrive. He had been there since ten o'clock. It was going on eleven-thirty. According to Ginny the plane should have landed already, and they should be arriving any minute. When Ginny had called him at the hotel to tell him that she, as well as Caitlin, would be coming and that they had gotten two cancellations for the same hotel, Julian could hardly believe it.

As he sat, watching the other students milling about, joking and laughing, and generally making fools of themselves, he felt like getting up and telling them what a group of juvenile idiots they were. He couldn't imagine Caitlin Ryan fitting in with that crowd.

Leaning his head against the rattan scrollwork of his chair back, he tried to picture how Caitlin would look when she arrived. Would she be cool and serene, even in this heat? Oh, yes. He could see her in a sophisticated white dress, her hair pulled back in a chignon, one of those large hats framing her face. No, no. That was all wrong. That was straight out of a fifties B movie, the kind that had been shown at the theater in Rock Ridge when he was a small boy. Those movies had been old even then. He rearranged the vision of her in his head. Perhaps she might be dressed—

But there she was!

At first he could hardly believe it was Caitlin. Something had happened over Christmas—something had changed her. He watched as she came into the lobby and crossed toward the reception desk—like an exploding star, trailing sparkles of energy in her wake. She was virtually dancing her way across, stopping to say hello to this boy, then on to flirt with that one, to laugh with another group. He was entranced anew. If he had thought Caitlin was lovely before, what was she now? No description could do her justice.

Ginny still felt tired as she followed Caitlin into the lobby. Not only did she feel hot and sleepy, she knew how terrible she must look. She just hoped she could get to the room she was sharing with Caitlin without running into Julian. She didn't want him to see her looking so rumpled. Suddenly she came to a halt, swallowing hard when she realized that Julian was practically right in front of her. He was only about twelve feet away, sitting in a fan-backed chair. He hadn't seen her yet. Quickly she looked around for a potted palm or something to hide behind. She settled for a brochure stand instead.

She peeked out from between a pamphlet on

Fort Lauderdale's attractions and a map of the beaches. God! He was so great looking. He looked as if he belonged in that hotel lobby—like some romantic hero from an early Hollywood movie. She could hardly wait for the party later on.

Ginny resolved to win him. She would get some sun, then shower and spend a lot of time getting her hair and makeup perfect.

As she watched Julian, she noticed that he was fascinated with someone—or something. She followed the line of his gaze, and she watched for several seconds. It was Caitlin. He couldn't take his eyes off her.

Caitlin!

Her heart sank. Well, why wouldn't he stare at her? Caitlin never seemed to be affected by rain or snow or hot, sticky weather. It was a good thing Caitlin was her best friend. If she weren't, Ginny knew she could become very jealous of her. Well, she would wait until that night, Ginny thought, when she would have Julian's full attention.

Ginny was beginning to wonder what was going on. The party had started two hours before. Dressed in her new lime green strapless sun dress, she knew she looked good—more than good. Caitlin had said so. Then why hadn't she gotten to dance with Julian more than once? And why was she standing next to the wall, feeling like a part of the flowered wallpaper? And why was Julian dancing with Caitlin for the seventh time in a row? Caitlin knew Ginny was over there, waiting for Julian. She had even seen Caitlin look over. Caitlin had signaled that she understood when Ginny had motioned toward Julian's back. But that had been twenty-five minutes before. Ginny felt like crying.

Julian pulled Caitlin closer. Then, with his hand firmly around her waist, he whirled her into an intricate step. She laughed gaily as she easily followed him, the full skirt of her yellow dress billowing out as they spun in place. Glancing over her shoulder, he saw, with tremendous satisfaction, all the covetous looks he was receiving from boys standing on the sidelines. Yes! He had the belle of the ball. And he wasn't about to let her go.

Bending his head so that his mouth was close to her ear, he said in a low, smooth voice, "I'm tired of being the object of so much envy. I can practically feel the looks of those poor boys slicing into my back. Why don't we get out of here for a while? I believe there's a small terrace just outside, through those doors over there.

And it leads to the beach. Perhaps we could walk along the sand for a bit."

Say yes, Caitlin, he beamed his thoughts at her. *Say yes. Because, if you do, it will only be a matter of time before you are mine to do with as I wish. And once I have, you will never be satisfied with Jed again. Nor will Jed want you. Say yes. Say yes.* He pulled her closer, gently rubbing the lower muscles of her back with the palm of his hand. He almost smiled as she responded automatically, arching toward him. "Shall we, Caitlin?"

"Yes—perhaps," she agreed softly. "It is warm in here."

Julian led her from the floor, keeping his arm around her waist. They walked past Ginny. He tried not to glance at her, but he did automatically. The look of hatred on her face was clear, even from the corner of his eye. *Poor Ginny,* he thought. Then he dismissed her.

When they reached the arched doorway that opened onto the night, he paused, then stopped Caitlin. "Wait here," he told her, first reaching up and gently pushing back the tiny tendrils of hair that clung damply at the pulse points of her temples. "I'll be right back."

Mesmerized by Julian's tenderness toward her, Caitlin gave a small nod of assent. She waited quietly as she watched him cross the dance floor to the bar that was set up in the corner. What was it about Julian that made her feel helpless? She sighed softly. He really was so handsome. She saw him coming back toward her, a glass of white wine in each hand.

"I thought you might like some. It's nice and chilled."

She smiled at him, and they moved through the door to the edge of the terrace. There was a low stone wall, actually the top of the seawall. They leaned against it, facing each other. Caitlin sipped at the wine and felt the warmth slide through her.

Below where they stood, low, slowly undulating waves washed in, receded, then came in again.

Caitlin sipped at the wine again. "I love that sparkling on the top of the waves. It's like hundreds of tiny green diamonds."

"It's called phosphorescence," Julian explained softly. Then raising a hand, he traced a line down the side of Caitlin's cheek, down her neck, and around to her back. "But I'd rather call it magic, wouldn't you?" He began to softly massage her back. Carefully he put his wineglass down on the top of the wall, then gently took hers and set it alongside his. "Come on. Let's walk down on the sand," he suggested.

They went down a set of steps. The moon had just risen, and Caitlin's eyes quickly adjusted to the moonlit darkness. She saw the spot where she had been lying earlier that afternoon, working on her tan. Bending down, she removed her shoes, keeping a hand on Julian's arm for balance. Carrying the shoes by their sling backs, she walked with him.

A beach chair, one of the large double ones, with a half umbrella over it for privacy, loomed up in front of them.

"It's very comfortable," Julian said. "I spent the afternoon in one. The cushions are deep. Here, sit down."

Before she knew it, Caitlin felt herself being gently lowered into the chair. And then Julian was sitting down beside her. "See," he said. "Now we can watch the magic of the waves in comfort." Julian slipped his arm around her shoulders, then pulled her to him. She relaxed her head into the hollow between his arm and chest. Her bare shoulders felt the warmth of his skin through his shirt. The intimate contact stirred her. She turned toward him. Then, in the darkness, his lips found hers. They were gentle as a sea breeze at first. But as the waves lapped at the shore, then withdrew their magic, then returned, the urgency of his lips increased. Caitlin found herself responding. Julian's hand moved down her back, pulling her closer. There was a hollow in the cushions, and he began to slide her ever so gently into it. Reaching up, Caitlin entwined her arms about his neck to pull him down with her. She felt his body start to

197

move over hers. Suddenly the realization of what was happening washed over her. And she felt a wave of loyalty toward Jed. She pushed at Julian's shoulders. "No. Oh, no, Julian. What am I doing? I can't—I can't do this."

"What can't you do, my love?" Julian whispered.

"This is wrong. I'm sorry. I'm so sorry." She pushed harder at his shoulders.

Julian was totally unprepared for her response. With her outburst, he released her, then sat up.

"Julian, I can't do this to you. You're too good. I don't love you, Julian. You're my friend—and a very good one. I didn't realize it until just this moment. I've allowed myself to dream, to feel as though I were in love this evening. It was wonderful, Julian, but it was wrong. Because it wasn't you I was thinking of when we were kissing."

"I see," Julian said thickly. In the dark he struggled to pull himself together. For a moment there, he had almost lost sight of the real purpose of the evening. With great self-discipline, he put his arm round her again, this time in a friendly way. "Of course, Caitlin, I understand."

"Oh, Julian." Caitlin put her head on his shoulder again. "You are such a wonderful, wonderful friend."

"I hope I always will be, Caitlin," Julian said

softly. Tentatively, very tentatively, he reached up to gently touch the side of her face. Without knowing it, he thought, Caitlin's response had helped him regain his self-control. With a shock, he realized, that for a short time he had been in great danger—in danger of falling in love.

Later that night, Caitlin lay awake in her bed at the hotel. As she stared up at the darkened ceiling, she thought about what had happened on the beach with Julian. It would have been wrong to let him make love to her, and she knew she had done the right thing. He was so kind and supportive, and Caitlin was sure that she would have been jeopardizing their friendship if she had used him to help her forget about Jed. Caitlin also knew that when she did give herself to a man, it would have to be someone she loved with all her heart. And she did not love Julian.

But, she realized with a start, he wasn't just a friend, either. Guys who were only friends didn't make you feel the way she felt when Julian had taken her into his arms. And friends didn't find themselves as attracted to each other the way she was attracted to Julian. But then what was he to her? How did he fit into her life? He was more than a friend, but less than a boyfriend. Would that change? Could she be falling in love with him?

The questions tumbled around in Caitlin's

mind, and she restlessly tossed and turned in her bed. She didn't have any answers. All she was really sure about was that her relationship with Jed was over, and that Julian was starting to mean more to her than she had ever thought he would.

FRANCINE PASCAL

In addition to collaborating on the Broadway musical *George M!* and the nonfiction book *The Strange Case of Patty Hearst*, Francine Pascal has written an adult novel, *Save Johanna!*, and four young adult novels, *Hangin' out With Cici*, *My First Love and Other Disasters*, *The Hand-Me-Down Kid*, and *Love and Betrayal & Hold the Mayo!* She is also the creator of the Sweet Valley High series. Ms. Pascal has three daughters, Jamie, Susan, and Laurie, and lives in New York City.

DIANA GREGORY

Growing up in Hollywood, Diana Gregory wanted to become an actress. She became an associate TV producer instead. Now a full-time writer, she has written, in addition to other books, three young adult novels, *I'm Boo! That's Who!*, *There's a Caterpillar in My Lemonade*, and *The Fog Burns Off by Eleven O'Clock*, plus several Sweet Dreams novels. Besides writing, her other love is traveling. She has lived in several states, including Virginia, where she stayed on a horse farm for a year. She now calls Seattle home.

A LOVE TRILOGY
First there is <u>LOVING</u>.

Meet Caitlin, gorgeous, rich charming and wild. And anything Caitlin wants she's used to getting. So when she decides that she wants handsome Jed Michaels, there's bound to be some trouble. ☐ 24716 $2.95

Then there is <u>LOVE LOST</u>.

The end of term has arrived and it looks like the summer will be a paradise. But tragedy strikes and Caitlin's world turns upside down. Will Caitlin speak up and risk sacrificing the most important thing in her life?
☐ 25130 $2.95

And at last, <u>TRUE LOVE</u>.

Things are just not going the way Caitlin had planned and she can't seem to change them! Will it take a disaster and a near-fatality for people to see the light?
☐ 25295/$2 95

<u>Prices and availability subject to change without notice.</u>

Buy them at your local bookstore or use this handy coupon for ordering: